HOWDY!

Welcome to the Circle C. My name is Andi Carter. If you are a new reader, here's a quick roundup of my family, friends, and adventures:

I'm a tomboy who lives on a huge cattle ranch near Fresno, California, in the exciting 1880s. I would rather ride my palomino mare, Taffy, than do anything else. I mean well, but trouble just seems to follow me around.

Our family includes my mother, Elizabeth, my ladylike older sister, Melinda, and my three older brothers: Justin (a lawyer), Chad, and Mitch. I love them, but sometimes they treat me like a pest. My father was killed in a ranch accident a few years ago.

In **Long Ride Home**, Taffy is stolen and it's my fault. I set out to find my horse and end up far from home and in a heap of trouble.

In **Dangerous Decision**, I nearly trample my new teacher in a horse race with my friend Cory. Later, I have to make a life-or-death choice.

Next, I discover I'm the only one who doesn't know the Carter **Family Secret**, and it turns my world upside down.

In **San Francisco Smugglers**, a flood sends me to school in the city for two months. My new roommate, Jenny, and I discover that the little Chinese servant-girl in our school is really a slave.

Trouble with Treasure is what Jenny, Cory, and I find when we head into the mountains with Mitch to pan for gold.

And then I may lose my beloved horse, Taffy, if I tell what I saw in **Price of Truth**.

Now saddle up and ride into my latest adventure!

Andi

ANDREA CARTER AND THE

Price of Truth

EDITION • 6

ANDREA CARTER AND THE

Price of Truth

SUSAN K. MARLOW

Kregel
Publications

Printed in the United States of America
19 20 21 22 23 24 25 26 / 5 4 3 2

CONTENTS

Chapter One

TOO MANY PEACHES

SAN JOAQUIN VALLEY, CALIFORNIA, SUMMER 1881

"Oh, no. Not again." Andi Carter watched in dismay as her bushel basket of plump, golden peaches toppled over and spilled to the ground.

"I told you this was a *loco* idea," her best friend, Rosa, grumbled in Spanish. "We should go back to the house before your brother catches us out here." She glanced around warily, as if Chad might pop out from behind a peach tree at any moment.

"No." Andi squatted next to the overturned basket, righted it, and began piling the ripened fruit back in. This was not the first basket of peaches she had ruined during the past three weeks, nor did she expect it would be her last. The full baskets were heavy and awkward to handle—especially for a girl barely turned thirteen. Even together, she and Rosa had a hard time lifting the fruit onto the flatbed wagons.

"Rodrigo threatened to fire us if we spoil any more fruit," Rosa said crossly. She made no effort to help Andi pick up the fuzzy golden balls scattered at her feet.

Andi paused and gave Rosa a quick smile. "He won't fire us." She brushed aside her long, dark braid and reached for another peach. "He needs every pair of hands he can hire."

"But he will scold us again. I do not wish to be yelled at by your brother's foreman." She gave Andi a pleading look. "Dressing up in my clothes and speaking Spanish might disguise you for a few weeks, but you cannot go unnoticed by the *capataz* forever. One of these days he will see who you are and then . . . how he will scold!"

9

Andi knew in her heart that Rosa spoke the truth. She should not have talked her friend into joining her in the orchard with the harvest hands. The girls' harvesting skills were an embarrassment to the other pickers, and the work was exhausting. It was only because Rodrigo was so shorthanded that he tolerated their presence at all.

"Can we *please* give up this idea and go home?" Rosa asked.

Andi sat back on her heels and pondered. It had seemed like such a splendid plan a few weeks ago, and the only way she could think of to earn some money of her own. And wasn't it for a good cause? For once in her life, Andi wanted to buy her mother a special birthday present with money she earned herself. She was tired of being just another name on the gift, scribbled in at the end. Often, she didn't even know what her older brothers and sister had bought—no one bothered to tell her. She was the little sister. Who cared what she thought?

Andi rose to her feet. "Not this year."

"*Cómo?*" Rosa wrinkled her brow.

"I was thinking about Mother's birthday," Andi said. "And I'm not quitting this job. I finally figured out one good thing about being the youngest in the family." With a practiced eye, she spied a ripe peach and yanked it from the branch.

"*Sí?*"

"With Mother away in San Francisco visiting Aunt Rebecca and Kate, no one pays me any mind—so long as I get my chores done. Justin's in town all day, Chad and Mitch are out on the range, and Melinda's so busy playing lady of the house that she doesn't ask how I spend my days." She grinned. "This money-making venture is working perfectly."

Rosa looked doubtful. "What would your mother say if she knew you were buying her gift with money you earned by working like a *peón* in your family's orchard?"

Andi lost her smile. "She wouldn't like it. That's why we're not going to tell anybody, remember? As soon as I earn enough money to buy that fancy music box I saw at the mercantile, I won't pick another peach." She settled the golden piece of fruit in the bushel basket and reached for the handle. "Here, let's try lifting it again."

Rosa grasped the other handle. Together they struggled to balance the load between them and walk at the same time. "Why do you not buy the music box with the reward money you got from returning the stolen bank gold this summer?" the Mexican girl asked.

Down went the basket, harder than it should considering the delicate load it contained. Three peaches rolled off and thudded to the ground.

"Because, like the nitwit I am, I put all the reward money in the bank," Andi said. "It's locked up tight. I can't draw out a penny of that fifty dollars without Mother's signature."

How stupid could I be? In her excitement to open a bank account of her own, Andi hadn't considered keeping any money back. She couldn't very well walk up to Mother at this late date and ask her to cosign. Mother might guess the reason her daughter suddenly wanted a little spending money. *I want her birthday gift to be a surprise.*

Rosa shrugged, which was her way of agreeing that Andi was a nitwit. She motioned to the basket. "*¡Pesa tanto!* How much farther is the wagon?"

Andi didn't know. She hoped it was nearby because Rosa spoke the truth. The basket *was* heavy. She cocked an ear and listened to the sounds of rustling branches and chattering voices. Faint laughter drifted on the breeze. "I think they left us behind again." She slid to the ground under a tree and yawned. "Maybe someone will come by and give us a hand."

As if in answer to her wish, the laughter Andi heard grew louder. Two young harvest hands emerged from behind the trees, whistling and joking with each other. When they saw the girls, they stopped.

"Ah, *chicas*," one of them said, "you are too slow. The *capataz* is not pleased. He has sent us to hurry you along."

Andi and Rosa jumped up and exchanged glances. Another scolding.

The other young man eyed their basket. "Of course you will need help to carry your heavy load, *no?*" He nudged his friend. "We are happy to do this, eh, Rico?"

"*Sí*, Carlos." Rico grinned. "It is our pleasure."

Andi felt a stab of uneasiness. On the surface the young men seemed eager to help, but there was something unsettling about their banter. Something that made Andi's heart beat faster. She looked at Rosa and saw her friend's face reflecting her own discomfort.

"*Vengan, chicas.*" Rico waved at the girls to come along. "We are wasting time." He nodded at Carlos, who swept up the girls' bushel basket with no effort and started walking away.

Andi and Rosa didn't move.

Still grinning, Rico took Rosa's arm and reached for Andi.

"I can walk by myself," Andi said in fluent Spanish, but Rico held her fast.

"*Señorita,*" he said with an amused twist of his lips, "please allow us to escort you back to Rodrigo. The *capataz* wishes to speak with you. I think you will be losing your place in the orchard after today."

Andi stopped struggling. "We're getting fired?"

Rico nodded. "*Sí*, but have no fear." His teeth gleamed in his dark face. "My brother and I told Rodrigo that we are your cousins, and you will stay with us from now on. We will see to it that you work hard and do not fall behind."

Andi met Rico's laughing eyes with a cold, blue stare. "You're not our cousins, and Rodrigo's *loco* if he believes such nonsense."

Rico shrugged good-naturedly. "Then he is *loco*."

Andi stopped short, catching Rico off guard. She kicked his shin with all her might and twisted free from his grip.

Rico yelped in pain.

Carlos, who had turned to watch, roared his laughter.

"Run, Rosa!" Andi grabbed her friend's hand. Together they

rammed into Carlos. He and the basket he was carrying crashed to the ground. Peaches rolled everywhere. Andi and Rosa scrambled over the top, slipping and sliding on the soft, squishy fruit. Without looking back, they fled.

They didn't get far.

Blocking their way stood the tall, formidable figure of the foreman, Rodrigo. His face darkened at the sight of the overturned bushel basket, Carlos covered in sticky peaches, and Rico moaning and rubbing his leg. "What is going on here?"

"*Nada,*" Carlos answered quickly. "Nothing at all. We were fetching our cousins as you asked us to do. They will be no more trouble, I assure you."

"They're no cousins of *mine,*" Andi burst out in English, too shaken and angry to realize her mistake. "They're just a couple of worthless—"

"*Silencio!*" Rodrigo shouted. Then his expression changed from anger to bewilderment. He narrowed his eyes and peered closely at Andi, who immediately dropped her gaze to the ground.

With a flick of his wrist, Rodrigo snatched the wide-brimmed *sombrero* from Andi's head. "No, *señorita*, I can see that they are no cousins of *yours.*" He turned to Rico and Carlos. "Get back to work. You've wasted enough time with your foolishness."

"But *capataz!*" Rico protested. "You asked us to—"

"*¡Váyanse!*"

Rodrigo's sharp command to get going sent the two men scrambling.

When they had disappeared between the peach trees, Andi looked at the foreman. "Rodrigo, I'm sorry, but—"

"No, *señorita.*" He held up his hand. "It is not to me you will explain. Now, come." He led them through the orchard until they arrived at the shack that served as the harvest foreman's office. "You will wait here." He motioned them into the shade behind the building.

Andi crumpled to the ground. "Please don't tell Chad."

Rodrigo pushed back his *sombrero* and gave Andi an incredulous look. "You ask me to disgrace myself by deceiving your brother—my employer?" He beckoned a young boy over.

"*¿Sí, Papá?*" The child listened to his father's instructions with wide eyes. "*¿Señor Chad? ¿Aquí? Sí, Papá.*" Then he scrambled onto the back of a small sorrel horse and dug his heels into its sides.

Within moments, the boy and his horse had disappeared between the rows of peach trees.

Andi watched the little boy gallop away. She hung her head. "There goes my job," she mumbled, "and Mother's birthday present."

Chapter Two

CHAD

A ndi leaned her head back against the rough planks of the shed and closed her eyes. An hour under the blistering August sun had drained away what little energy remained after being discovered by Rodrigo. The tiny slice of shade she and Rosa occupied offered no relief from the heat. Sweat trickled freely down Andi's back, plastering her once-white cotton blouse to her skin.

A *plunk* caught Andi's attention, and she opened her eyes. A few yards away a ripe peach lay under a tree. A gust of hot wind brushed by her, and another peach plopped to the ground. Although her throat was dry as dust and her stomach rumbled, Andi didn't touch the fruit. Instead, she contented herself with a drink from the canteen Rodrigo had brought them. The warm, stale water slid down her throat.

She splashed some water over her head and passed the canteen to Rosa. "I never thought Rodrigo could be so heartless," she complained. "I don't see why we can't wait inside."

Andi didn't ask him though. Beneath the foreman's stiff formality toward her, she sensed a seething rage. He kept them in sight at all times, as if he knew she'd grab Rosa and run the first chance she got.

If I thought I could outrun him, I would. But he'd catch me before I made it to Taffy.

Rosa didn't say a word. She sat ramrod straight, clearly terrified out of her wits.

15

Andi picked up a rock and chucked it at the closest peach. "Why are *you* so scared? You've got every right to work in our orchard if you want to." She picked up another rock.

"I told you this was a bad idea," Rosa said. "*Rodrigo está furioso. Señor* Chad will yell and yell."

Andi cringed. Rodrigo was furious, all right. Rosa was right about Chad too. When her brother was angry, he could really holler. "Chad will yell at *me*, not you. It's Andrea Carter who can't work where she likes, or when she likes, or anything!"

She hurled the rock at the peach and scowled when she missed her target. What was taking Chad so long? Why was Rodrigo making her sit out here in the heat when she could be home, resting behind the cool, thick stucco walls of the ranch house?

Whatever the reason, Andi had plenty of time to brood over her actions of the past few weeks. All her plans to buy her mother's gift were crumbling. The sensible thing would be to ask Justin for the money. She knew her oldest and favorite brother would help her out.

Why can't I accept a favor? Why, instead, do I always end up doing crazy things that land me in trouble?

She sighed. "No matter how hard I try, I'm always in some kind of fix."

Rosa didn't deny it. She gave a small smile and said, "Ah, but your heart is kind."

"But not always connected to my head," Andi admitted. "Remember the time I ran off and Taffy was stolen?"

Rosa nodded. "But if you had not been searching for your horse, you would not have met me or helped my family find work. Your ranch is the best place we ever worked."

"What about that race with Cory last fall? It seemed like so much fun, until I trampled the new teacher."

Rosa shook her head. "No, that was not so good. Trouble does seem to follow you, but I think it is because you have so many unexpected ideas. You do them without thinking and—"

16

"I usually end up in a heap of trouble. Just like this time." Silently she added, *Because I want to do things myself, without being treated like a little kid.* When would everyone figure that out? Hadn't she proved she was grown up when she saved her brother's life this summer? She winced. *But I told Mitch I didn't want to grow up.*

Everything was so mixed up.

"I don't know what I want," she muttered. She pitched another rock. This one found its target. *Splat!* The peach burst open.

A few minutes later, Chad rode up. Andi peeked around the corner. She was almost glad to see him. Nothing, she decided, could be worse than sitting on the dusty ground, roasting in the heat, bored to death, and squirming under the watchful gaze of the Carters' harvest foreman.

She was wrong.

"Rodrigo!" Chad dismounted and ground-tied his horse. "What in blazes is so urgent that it can't wait for this evening's report?" He yanked off his hat and wiped the sweat from his forehead. "Your boy wouldn't give me any details. I was clear out at—"

"*Señor*," Rodrigo interrupted. He held up his hand to forestall further outbursts. "I apologize for pulling you away from your work, but this is a matter that could not wait. If you would follow me, please." Without another word, he led Chad around to the back of the shack and pointed to the two girls sitting in the narrow strip of shade.

Andi sprang to her feet, as did Rosa.

Chad's mouth fell open. Before he could speak, Rodrigo began to express his annoyance in a stream of sizzling Spanish. It was worded respectfully, but neither Andi nor Chad had any doubt that the foreman intended to let his employer know exactly what he thought.

"This is no place for your sister, *señor*. Many shiftless, no-account *hombres* are lurking about the orchards this season, as you well know." Rodrigo went on to describe the improper advances two of the workers had made toward the girls. "I cannot watch her every moment or be responsible for her safety," he finished with a grunt. "You must keep her away from here."

Chad nodded wordlessly. He looked dazed.

Rodrigo had no problem filling the silence. "I apologize, *señor*, for not noticing her earlier. I have not taken the time to acquaint myself with the harvest hands. If something bad had happened to her, I would have myself to blame."

Chad swept Rodrigo's apology aside and found his voice. "You did exactly right, Rodrigo. *Muchas gracias.* You're a good foreman—one of my best—and your concern for Andi's safety proves it. I promise you this will *not* happen again."

"What about this one?" Rodrigo indicated Rosa, who trembled and stared at the ground.

Chad turned to Andi. "How did you two get out here?"

"On Taffy," Andi whispered.

"Tagging around with Andi all day is punishment enough," Chad told Rosa. "Find Taffy and take her home." He slapped his hat against his leg and slammed it down on his head. "Andi will ride with me."

Rosa took off like a shot without an *adiós* or a backward glance.

Chad crooked a finger at his sister. "Let's go."

Andi followed Chad to his horse and mounted up behind him. Any second she expected her brother to explode, but he urged his horse into a swinging lope and ignored her.

Just yell at me and get it over with! she pleaded silently. Perhaps he was waiting until they rode into the yard, so he could yell at her in front of the ranch hands. *That would be just like him*, she thought in disgust. But right now she was too hot and too tired to care.

The sudden jerk from lope to walk startled Andi. She clutched her brother's waist to keep her seat.

"What were you doing out there?" he asked.

Andi didn't answer.

"You're not going to tell me?"

"I can't."

"Can't? Or *won't*?"

Andi paused. Would it be so terrible to tell him her secret plan to surprise their mother? After all, he loved Mother too. He'd understand. Or would he? It was more likely he'd brush off her idea as just another one of her silly notions—which wasn't too far from the truth.

I don't want him teasing me, or telling me I'm being foolish. Besides, knowing Chad, there was always the possibility that he'd slip and reveal the surprise. She couldn't take that chance.

Chad brought his horse to a full stop and turned around. "You better tell me. With Mother gone and Justin in town most days, it's fallen on me to watch out for you." His fingers tightened around the reins. "By the look of things, I haven't done a very good job of it."

It was no trick for Andi to figure out that her brother was frustrated. She'd done it again—plunged wholeheartedly into what she thought was a wonderful idea, only to discover her plans were full of deep, dark holes. Rosa had warned her. Would she never learn?

Chad was still talking, but he didn't sound angry anymore. Leastways, he wasn't yelling. "How could I have faced Mother if . . . those . . . if you'd gotten hurt out there?"

Andi reddened. She knew Chad was remembering what Rodrigo had told him about the two harvest hands they'd met up with today. "I'm sorry, Chad," she relented. "I just wanted to earn a little money of my own."

Chad's eyebrows rose. "What do you need money for?"

Andi scowled. Nope. She would not tell him that—even if she *was* sorry she'd frightened him. Quickly, she changed the subject. "Are you going to telegraph Mother?"

Chad nudged the horse, and they continued on their way. "I'm not going to worry Mother. I'm not even going to yell at you. Scolding you can't rid me of the cold, sick feeling in my gut whenever I think about what could have happened to you." He shook his head. "You

went too far this time, little sister. You deliberately deceived my foreman and put yourself in danger—for a few dollars."

"I didn't think it was dangerous to pick a few peaches from our
own orchard."

"You are welcome to ride out to the orchard and ask Rodrigo for
as many peaches as you like," Chad told her coldly, "but you will
go out there as *Andrea Carter*—properly escorted and treated with
respect as part of this family—not disguised as a harvest hand. And
you will not pick fruit. Have I made myself clear?"

Andi bowed her head. "Yes, Chad."

"Good. See that you don't forget."

Andi bristled at the restriction but kept her mouth shut. It didn't
seem right. Rosa could pick peaches and earn a little spending
money, but not Andi. She mentally kicked herself for putting all
of the reward money in the bank. Well, perhaps there was a way of
getting it out.

She set her jaw. She would get the money she needed if it was the
last thing she ever did. And nobody was going to find out about it
until they gathered for the party at the beginning of October. Her
entire family, and especially her mother, would get the biggest surprise of their lives when they saw the music box.

Andi wasn't quite sure how she was going to accomplish this—
yet. *There are more ways to catch a calf than by tossing a rope over its
head,* she decided as they rode into the yard.

Chapter Three

THE MUSIC BOX

It was no use asking Chad for the money Andi had earned in the orchard. Keeping it was most likely his way of punishing her for going out there in the first place. Three whole weeks wasted! School would be starting in another week, and she was no closer to buying her mother's birthday present than she'd been at the beginning of the harvest.

But two days after the disaster in the orchard, Chad took Andi aside after breakfast. He dropped four shiny coins in her hand and said, "Here's your pay. I settled up with Rodrigo last night."

A five-dollar gold piece and three silver dollars! Andi opened her eyes wide with surprise. She fingered the coins in a mixture of guilt and gratitude, not knowing what to say. Finally, she looked up. Chad wasn't smiling, but he wasn't scowling either. "You're paying me?"

"Why wouldn't I? You did the work—although Rodrigo was sorely tempted to take all the peaches you damaged out of your pay. He says we have a reputation to uphold, and you spoiled more Carter fruit in three weeks than the rest of the harvest hands usually damage during an entire season." He crossed his arms over his chest and gave her the ghost of a smile. "I convinced him to let the matter go. If Rodrigo had his way, you'd be owing *me* money."

Andi returned her gaze to the shiny gold and silver pieces lying in her palm. Her spirits rose, and a smile tugged at her lips. "Thanks, Chad," she murmured, closing her hand securely around the coins.

Before her brother could ask any probing questions about Andi's plans for the money, she sprinted toward the stairs. She passed Melinda, who wanted to know where she was off to in such a hurry.

"I'm going to town," Andi replied breathlessly from the top of the stairs. "Soon as I change into riding clothes."

"No, you're not," Melinda said. "You're not supposed to ride into town alone."

"I won't be alone," Andi shot back. "Rosa's going with me."

Before Melinda could protest, Andi ducked into her room to change.

"There it is, Rosa. What do you think?" Andi leaned her forehead against the plate-glass window of the mercantile and peered beyond Mr. Goodwin's ever-present *Help Wanted* sign. She absently twisted the end of one long, dark braid. "Isn't it the most beautiful music box you ever saw?"

"Oh *sí*, Andi! It is very nice, but . . ." Rosa's voice trailed off.

"But what?" Andi pulled her gaze away from the display window and saw a puzzled look in her friend's dark, expressive eyes.

Rosa lifted her palms in confusion. "What is this . . . *music box*? For many days in the orchard you tell me about this wonderful box that plays music, but"—she pointed toward the window—"now I see only a small box. A pretty one, *sí*, but how does it play music?"

"You wind it up with a little key, and when you open the lid, music comes out. There's a tube inside that goes around and makes it play."

Rosa smiled her approval. "A lovely gift for the *señora*. She will like it very much, I think. How much does it cost?"

Andi sighed. "I don't know." With hesitant fingers, she reached into the pocket of her dark-blue riding skirt and drew out the money from Chad. What had seemed like a lot of money this morning now looked woefully inadequate to pay for such a fine music box. "What if it costs more than I have?"

Rosa eyed the coins. "Go inside and ask how much it costs."

Andi shoved the coins back in her pocket. "I can't. I'm afraid it'll be too expensive."

"Excuse me, ladies. Is there something I can help you find?"

Andi spun around at the sound of a deep voice coming from nearby. Mr. Goodwin, the shop's owner, stood in the doorway of the mercantile, holding a broom.

"H-howdy, Mr. Goodwin," Andi stammered. A flush warmed her cheeks. She'd been caught staring into the store's large window like a poor street urchin.

Mr. Goodwin smiled in recognition, leaned his broom against the doorjamb, and joined them. He peered over Andi's shoulder into his display window. "Something catch your eye, Andi, or are you just window shopping?"

"Actually," Andi began, "I—"

"She would like to see the box that plays music," Rosa said with a sly smile.

Andi gaped at her friend. Although Rosa's English had improved greatly over the past year, it wasn't often she felt confident enough to speak to strangers—especially to a shopkeeper.

"Lovely, isn't it?" Mr. Goodwin remarked. "Of course, it's not as fancy as some you'd find in San Francisco, but it's not as costly either. Quite a few young ladies have been admiring it these past few weeks."

The words *not as costly* sent a surge of hope through Andi.

"Why don't you come inside and take a closer look?" Mr. Goodwin invited.

Andi nodded, and she and Rosa followed him into the store. Reaching over a display of kerosene lamps and ivory-handled hairbrushes, Mr. Goodwin lifted the music box from its place near the front of the window. "Here you are." He placed it in Andi's outstretched hands.

Andi cradled the box as gently as she would a newly hatched chick. Carefully, she raised the lid.

"Watch," Mr. Goodwin said. He turned the tiny key a few times and "Brahms' Lullaby" poured out, high and sweet.

Andi listened to the melody while she examined the small wooden box. She ran her fingers across the smooth rosewood pattern of leaves and flowers intricately inlaid in the dark, polished wood. It felt like satin.

Smiling, she closed the lid. The music stopped. She looked up at Mr. Goodwin. "It's exactly what I want, Mr. Goodwin. How much does it cost?" She held her breath and flicked a hopeful glance toward Rosa.

Rosa muttered, *"Imposible."*

"Is it more than eight dollars?" Andi blurted.

"I'm afraid so," Mr. Goodwin said.

"How much more?"

"I'm sorry, Andi. It's ten dollars and ninety-five cents."

"Ten dollars and ninety-five cents," Andi repeated softly. Her heart sank. "It might as well be a million."

"I'm sorry. Really I am."

Andi shrugged. "I guess we'd better be going. Thank you for showing it to us." With a sigh of regret, she returned the precious music box to Mr. Goodwin and headed out the door. "Come on, Rosa."

"¡Ay! It is a shame you cannot buy it." Then Rosa's eyes lit up. "Perhaps you will have enough money by Christmas. You could give it to the *señora* then."

Andi slumped against the doorpost. Rosa made it sound so easy.

But how can I earn money? Chad didn't pay her to take care of Taffy or clean out her stall. Chores were part of living on a ranch. Everybody did their share.

The ranch hands got wages, but Andi never asked for pay on those rare occasions when Chad allowed her to join him and Mitch with roundup or branding. *If I asked for pay, Chad would laugh and send me home.*

Andi sighed and glanced down J Street. Not far away, the Fresno County Bank took up an entire corner. She frowned. More money than she could ever need was right there, less than a block away. *Her* money. If there were only some way—

A daring idea flashed through her mind. *Well, why not?*

It was worth a try. All they could say was no. And maybe they'd say yes. She took a deep breath and pushed away from the post. "Come on, Rosa. We're going to the bank."

Rosa shot a quick glance at the large building then looked at Andi. "How does this help?"

"I've got fifty dollars sitting over there. I should be able to withdraw a little of it."

"But you said . . ." Rosa's voice trailed away at Andi's determined look.

"It doesn't hurt to ask." She turned and called into the open doorway of the mercantile, "I'll be right back, Mr. Goodwin. Don't sell that music box to anybody else in the next fifteen minutes."

"Oh, I won't." He joined Andi and followed her determined gaze. "You figurin' on holding up the bank?"

"Something like that." Andi stepped boldly off the boardwalk and into the dusty street.

Chapter Four

THREE DOLLARS SHORT

The three-story Fresno County Bank towered over most of the other buildings along J Street. Andi marched straight toward it, ignoring Rosa's groan of protest.

"Come on," Andi coaxed when they had crossed the street.

Rosa shook her head. Her two shiny black braids went flying. *"¡Yo no!* You should not either. No one will let you take money out of the bank, not without the *señora* along. This is another *loco* idea."

Andi was forced to agree. But she was also desperate. She stepped onto the boardwalk in front of the bank and repeated, "It's my money. Come on."

Rosa found a bench alongside the building and sat down. "I will wait outside the bank, if you please."

Andi did *not* please. She didn't want to enter the bank alone. *"Por favor?"* she pleaded.

Rosa flicked a piece of lint from her colorful skirt. Then she folded her hands and looked up at Andi. "I will wait here for you."

Andi let out an annoyed breath. Rosa usually went along with Andi's ideas, but sometimes her Mexican friend put her foot down and turned stubborn.

This was one of those times.

"Suit yourself." Andi turned the doorknob and stepped into the richly furnished bank lobby before she could change her mind.

Always before, Mother or Justin had been with her. Now she felt as if she'd stormed uninvited into the governor's mansion in Sacramento.

Young men in black suits with high, stiff collars nodded politely at customers. Their heels clicked on the shiny wood floor and echoed in the vast, high-ceilinged lobby. Other men sat behind large mahogany desks and murmured to wealthy matrons or overall-clad farmers.

Andi tiptoed to the shortest line. Just ahead of her, a loud, overdressed woman carried on a one-sided conversation with the bank teller trapped behind his barred window. The woman related her family history—including all the loved ones she'd lost over fifteen years ago during the War Between the States.

"Yes, ma'am." The young clerk forced a smile. "Now, all I need is your signature and we can complete your withdrawal."

"Yes, of course." There was a brief pause and the *scratch, scratch* of a pen tip against paper. "Now if the South had given command of the forces at Vicksburg to my dear Ambrose . . ." She prattled on.

Andi sighed. The line behind her began to grow.

"I'm sure you're right, Mrs. Fletcher. Here you are. Good day." The teller shook his head at the retreating figure.

Andi stepped up to the cage. Her heart was pounding, but she gave the clerk a bright smile. "Good morning. I'd like to withdraw ten dollars from my account."

The clerk stared at her.

"I said I'd like to—"

"I heard you." He frowned. "Children do not simply walk into this establishment and ask for money. Run along home and come back with your parents." He motioned to the woman standing behind Andi. "I can help you right here, Mrs. Perry."

"But . . ." Andi's face burned.

Mrs. Perry swished past Andi without so much as a nod.

"I'll help you, Andi." A handsome young man with brown hair and warm brown eyes smiled at her. He settled himself behind the empty teller's cage to Andi's left and waved her over.

Andi grinned. Peter Wilson was her brother Mitch's best friend. The two boys had grown up together and still enjoyed each other's company when time and work allowed. Andi had often tagged along behind Mitch and Peter when she was small, and Peter was always patient with her. He would certainly help her withdraw her money. He probably wouldn't even ask if her mother needed to sign anything.

"Howdy, Peter." Andi put her face close to the bars and whispered, "Does your father know how rude that fellow behind the next window is?"

"Who? Leo Frantz? He's one of Father's best cashiers."

"Ha! You'd think the bank president would expect his employees to be polite to everybody. That teller treated me like I was trying to hold up the bank."

"Never mind, Andi. Leo is a real stickler for the rules. I'll help you today, on one condition."

"What's that?"

"Tell me how Mitch is doing. Since his accident up in the mountains, I haven't seen him much. He didn't show up for the Fourth of July celebration last month. How's his leg?"

"Right as rain," Andi said. "His gunshot wound healed up fine. But Chad's got him so busy right now that Mitch hasn't any time for himself."

"I guess I'll have to ride out and convince Chad to let Mitch sneak away for a few days. You know what they say about all work and no play."

"You better be careful, or Chad will put *you* to work. You any good with cattle?" She gave him a teasing smile. What Peter knew about ranching wouldn't fill Mother's thimble.

Peter laughed. "The only time a steer and I see eye-to-eye is when it's lying on my plate as a thick, juicy steak." Then he turned businesslike. "So, Miss Carter, what brings you to the bank today?"

"I need money," Andi confessed. "Ten dollars." She swallowed.

Might as well make it worth my while and take out a little extra. No sense keeping so much of it stuck in a bank.

"Ten dollars," Peter repeated doubtfully.

"I have my own account," Andi said. "I opened it with my share of the reward money earlier this summer. Don't you remember? Now I need to draw some out." She leaned her arms on the counter and lowered her voice. "It's for a birthday present for my mother, but don't tell anybody, especially not Mitch. It's a surprise."

Peter winked. "Your secret's safe with me." He passed a slip of paper under the bars, along with a freshly dipped pen. "Sign here and I'll see what I can do."

Andi snatched up the pen and scrawled her name on the dotted line. She filled in the amount she wanted to withdraw and shoved the pen and paper to Peter.

"I'll be right back," he promised.

Andi chewed on her lip while she waited. All those long, hot days working in the orchard—not to mention getting on Rodrigo's bad side and worrying Chad—had been for nothing. With one swipe of the pen, she would soon have more than enough money to pay for the music box.

Her heart leaped with joy and relief. Peter was a good friend.

A few minutes later a red-faced Peter returned. Instead of bringing the ten dollars, the young man had brought his father, the bank president.

Andi swallowed. *Uh-oh.*

Mr. Charles Wilson was an older version of his son, but taller and heavier. He adjusted his wire spectacles over his nose, gave Andi a thin smile, and pushed the slip of paper toward her. "Miss Carter, I cannot withdraw funds from your account without your mother's signature."

Andi looked helplessly at Peter.

He gave her an apologetic shrug. "I'm sorry, Andi. I tried."

Andi hung her head. Her plan had failed. Once again she regretted her decision to put her reward money in the bank. How had she gotten talked into opening an account, anyway?

I should have kept it all at home in my treasure box. "It's *my* money, Mr. Wilson," Andi said. "Not my mother's. You know it's mine."

Mr. Wilson nodded. "You are correct, but that doesn't change anything." His voice softened. "Take the withdrawal slip home for your mother to sign, and stop by again tomorrow. I'll have your money waiting for you."

"But that would ruin the surprise. Besides, Mother's not home. She's gone to the city and won't be back 'til Saturday. Could I maybe have *three* dollars?"

Mr. Wilson frowned. "No, I'm sorry."

"Andi and her friends brought back your stolen bank money, Father," Peter said. "You can't let her have three dollars from her account?"

"No exceptions." He held his son's gaze. "You should know better than to question a bank policy." He held up a finger. "One exception, Peter, and word leaks out . . ." Mr. Wilson left his sentence unfinished and nodded toward the door. "Now, Andrea, please step aside and allow these other folks to conduct their business."

Andi fumed. She crumpled the paper into a tiny ball and jammed it into her pocket. Then she spun on her heel and marched out of the bank. She wanted to slam the door, but she stopped herself just in time. No matter how angry she was, Mother had taught her to be polite.

Andi slumped on the bench next to Rosa. She rested her elbows on her knees and propped her chin in her hands.

"You did not get the money."

Rosa's knowing smile brought Andi's temper to the boiling point. "No, I did not get the money! I'm thirteen years old—old enough to be earning wages—but everybody still treats me like a little kid. Chad won't let me work in the orchards or be a cowhand for pay. Mother won't let me take money from my account without her signature."

She blew out a long, frustrated breath. "So, Rosa, how am I ever going to earn another three dollars in less than a month without anybody at home finding out?"

"Perhaps you can find a job in town," Rosa suggested. "Your friend Rachel sews for the dressmaker sometimes, and Seth Atkins sells firewood. Maybe Widow Lawson needs—"

Andi leaped from the bench. "Rosa, you're brilliant! *¡Qué idea!* A job in town would be perfect. Nobody at home has to know about it. What about that *Help Wanted* sign in the window of the mercantile? I paid it no mind earlier, but now I'm going to ask Mr. Goodwin if he'll hire me to help around the store."

"But school begins next week," Rosa said. "How will you find the time?"

Andi smiled, her good temper restored. "Easy. Justin's been working late all month. If he keeps it up, I'll have a free hour every day after school. We have to wait for him to take us home anyway. I might as well be earning money." She left the boardwalk and crossed the dusty street.

Rosa ran to catch up.

"Mr. Goodwin!" Andi raced into the mercantile.

The storekeeper stepped out from behind the counter. "Oh, it's you again. How did the robbery go?"

"Not very well. I got caught." She pointed toward the window. "I saw your *Help Wanted* sign. Do you think I could work for you? I could stock shelves and sweep the floor and run errands. Anything you need."

Mr. Goodwin rubbed the back of his neck. "Well . . . I don't know, Andi. It's not like your folks need the money. What would your mother say?"

"She won't mind."

"You go along and ask her, and let me know tomorrow."

Andi felt trapped. "Uh, I can't do that." Before Mr. Goodwin could interrupt, Andi plunged ahead. "I told you earlier the music box is a surprise. If Mother finds out I'm working, she'll wonder why, and the surprise will be ruined. I've got eight dollars already. I picked peaches."

She reached into her pocket and pulled out the coins. "It's not like you'd have to hire me permanently or anything. Just for a few weeks—a month at the most. I could work an hour every day after school."

"I see," Mr. Goodwin said softly. He scratched his chin and glanced around the store.

Andi followed his gaze. She couldn't help noticing the thin layer of dust that covered the countertops. Goods on the shelves looked like they'd been stacked in a hurry and in no particular order. Crumbs littered the floor around the cracker barrel, and the candy jars were only half filled.

It was easy to see why Mr. Goodwin had hung the *Help Wanted* sign in his window.

"You won't be sorry if you hire me," Andi said in a rush. "Please?"

Mr. Goodwin chuckled. "All right, Andi. I'll help you out. I'll take your eight dollars on account and let you work off the rest." He let out a sigh. "Truth is, I need the help, and it's a relief not to have to pay you in cash money."

Andi squealed her delight. "Thank you, Mr. Goodwin!" She clasped his hand and shook it until the man laughed and gently pulled away.

A loud banging from the back of the store brought the three of them around. Mr. Goodwin's fourteen-year-old son, Jack, burst through the door from the living quarters and came around the counter. Without a word, he swaggered past them and headed for the jar of licorice.

"Jack," Mr. Goodwin prompted. "Your manners."

Jack stopped and glared.

"Howdy, Jack." Andi was surprised to see how tall he'd grown over the summer. She hadn't seen him since early June, when they'd spent an unhappy hour together in jail for accidentally wrecking the watering trough in front of the mercantile. "You and Cory been fishing much this summer?"

"Some," Jack replied. He helped himself to the candy and left the store.

An uncomfortable silence fell.

What's eating him? Andi wondered. She and Jack had been friends for years.

Mr. Goodwin cleared his throat. "You can see why I put up the sign," he offered in explanation. "Jack's been downright uncooperative this summer. He thinks it's beneath his dignity to work here and prefers to spend his time going around with Johnny Wilson." He snorted his opinion of the banker's son.

Andi caught her breath. Fifteen-year-old Johnny Wilson was a bully and a braggart who had plagued Andi and her classmates for years. The schoolmaster barely kept him under control. What did Jack see in *him*? "I'm sure sorry to hear that, Mr. Goodwin," she finally said.

Mr. Goodwin waved her sympathy away. Then he brightened. "You and Jack always got along real well. Perhaps you can convince him that associating with Johnny will only lead to trouble. He might listen to you. He doesn't listen to me these days."

Andi bit her lip and said nothing. A chill settled in her stomach. Mr. Goodwin expected *her* to talk to Jack? Now that he was spending time with Johnny, Jack wouldn't listen to anybody.

Especially not to Andi Carter.

Chapter Five

ENCOUNTER WITH A BULLY

Andi wandered down the wooden sidewalk with mixed feelings. On the one hand, she couldn't be happier. Her eight dollars were safely in the hands of Paul Goodwin and she had a job to work off the balance. Her mother's birthday gift was within reach. On the other hand, she had Jack's new attitude to contend with. She didn't look forward to working alongside him, but perhaps he wouldn't be around.

Either way, it was going to be a long month.

She shook herself free of her thoughts and turned to Rosa. "You've got to promise not to tell anybody about my job. It's our secret, right? My mother is going to be the most surprised person in the entire—"

A terrified shriek yanked Andi from her chatter. She clutched Rosa's arm. "What was *that?*"

Rosa's eyes opened wide. "*No sé.* It came from over there." She pointed to an alley running between Goodwin's Mercantile and the hardware store.

Another cry split the air, followed by harsh laughter. Andi leaped from the boardwalk and raced around the corner of the building.

"Andi, where are you going?" Rosa's exasperated shout went unheeded.

The alley between the stores was dim and narrow, crowded with large barrels and crates. Piles of scrap lumber and used bricks hugged the outside walls of the buildings. An old, broken wagon with a missing wheel lay across part of the alley. From behind the wagon came another frantic yelp.

"Your pa's nothing but a dirty, lazy drunk!" a cruel voice taunted.

Andi heard the sound of ripping cloth, followed by the muffled sobs of a small child. The pitiful crying tore through her heart and propelled her down the alley without a thought for her own safety.

She jumped over a crate and hurried to the other side of the wagon. Her breath caught in her throat, and she stopped short. Johnny Wilson and Jack Goodwin had cornered a little boy no more than seven or eight years old. His shirt was torn, his pants patched and ragged. The child huddled against the back wall of Goodwin's store, clenching his small fists. Tears streaked his dirty face.

"Let him go!" Andi shouted.

Jack and Johnny whirled. They stared at Andi in open-mouthed astonishment.

"You ought to be ashamed of yourselves." She shoved past the older boys and knelt beside the boy. "Run, Robbie," she said, helping him to his feet. "Don't stop 'til you get home."

Robbie wiped his nose and scampered away without a backward glance.

Andi watched the little boy until he was safely out of sight. Then she rose and faced Johnny and Jack. They hadn't moved. "Bullies," she muttered.

Her words brought Johnny to life. He nudged Jack and took two steps toward Andi, blocking her way. "What business do you have butting in like that?"

Andi paused, suddenly uneasy. Johnny's voice slammed home the recklessness of what she had just done. Johnny Wilson was trouble—serious trouble—and she had charged in and upset his plans. He was not likely to forget it. She looked around for Rosa, but her friend was nowhere in sight.

Johnny gripped her arm. "I asked you a question."

In spite of her racing heart, Andi stood tall. "I couldn't let you hurt Robbie. He's just a little boy. What's he ever done to you?" She tried to pry Johnny's fingers from her arm, but it was no use. "Your manners leave a lot to be desired. Let me go this instant."

She wondered, not for the first time, how two brothers could look so much alike but act so differently. Peter Wilson, the bank cashier, was the nicest young man Andi knew. His younger brother was the terror of the town.

Johnny gave Andi a cocky grin, but he didn't let her go. "The drunk's kid was stealing from the mercantile again. We caught him in the storeroom and decided to teach him a lesson."

Andi couldn't believe her ears. "By beating him up?"

"Yeah," Jack said. "Ben Decker and his kids are a disgrace to this town. Somebody should run 'em out."

Andi glared at Jack, who only a couple of months ago had been her friend. "That's the sheriff's business, not yours."

Johnny tightened his grip on Andi's arm. "It's none of your affair either, Miss High-and-Mighty Carter." His dark brown eyes glinted with anger. "You should have gone about your business and left well enough alone."

"I'll do as I like," Andi snapped. Johnny didn't scare her. Not much, anyway. "Now, let . . . me . . . go. *Or else.*"

"Or else *what?*" Johnny scowled. "You stick your nose in the air whenever I come around. You could be nicer to me, you know. I've never done anything to you."

It was true. Johnny tormented Andi's school chums by pulling their hair, slipping frogs and lizards down their backs, and chanting mean and untrue ditties for the entire schoolyard to hear. He tripped the girls skipping rope and chased the others with snakes. But Johnny limited his attacks on Andi to an occasional spit wad in class and a yank on her braids.

She knew why. "My brothers would skin you alive if you pestered me. Now let go. You're hurting me."

"Maybe you'd better leave off," Jack said. His gaze darted around the narrow alley. "I don't want to tangle with any of her brothers."

"Shut up, Jack," Johnny barked over his shoulder.

Jack ducked his head and backed away.

Andi squirmed. "You're a bully, Johnny Wilson. A horrid, nasty bully. You even bully your friends—the few that you have. That's why I stay away from you. You just wait. One of these days somebody's going to make you pay for all your meanness."

"Who? You?" With a laugh, Johnny freed her.

Andi rubbed her arm. "Oh, yes. If I got the chance, I sure would."

Johnny shook his head. "Andi, you are the sassiest girl I know. You're not like the rest of the simpering, squealing girls in this town. You got fire." He jammed his fists on his hips. "You should see yourself—sputtering at me like an angry chipmunk."

A *chipmunk*? Johnny was making fun of her!

"I won't hold your sass against you, of course. It's part of your"— Johnny grinned—"charm. Shall we call a truce? I'm really not such a bad fellow once you get to know me. We could even become friends." He winked. "What do you say?"

Andi stepped back, astonished. Johnny was as unpredictable as a stormy sea. One minute he acted like he despised her. The next minute he wanted to be . . . *friends*? What kind of friends?

At that moment, Andi couldn't think of a worse fate than to be friends with Johnny, especially the kind of friend he might be suggesting. "I'd sooner be friends with a rattlesnake."

Johnny jerked back as though slapped. "You Carters. Always too good for anybody. Well, Andrea Carter, you need to be taken down a peg."

"I'd like to see you try!" Andi burst out without thinking.

The look on Johnny's face told Andi she should have kept her mouth shut, but it was too late to take back her hasty words.

Johnny reacted instantly. He reached out, grabbed Andi by the shoulders, and planted a hurried but firm kiss on her lips. Then he smirked. "You're not so high and mighty now, I bet."

Andi gasped. A hot flush crept up her neck and exploded in her cheeks. Her stomach knotted. Never in her wildest imagination would she have guessed that Johnny could be such a cad, such a—

Whack! She slammed her fist smack into Johnny's sneering face.

"Augh!" Johnny covered his nose and staggered backward. He stumbled, lost his footing, and crashed to the ground. Shock replaced his usual cocky grin.

Andi's knuckles burned, but it was worth it. How dare a boy—*any* boy—show such appalling behavior! Johnny was a bully, but he came from a good family.

He knew better.

Johnny slowly took his hand away from his nose and stared at the bright red blood dripping from his fingers. "You . . . you . . ."

"J-Johnny Wilson," Andi stammered, "you are the most ill-bred and disgusting boy I know. If it's the last thing I ever do, I'll pay you back for shaming me like this. You just wait and see."

Johnny lurched to his feet, swiping at his bloody nose. He clearly didn't want to be friends with Andi any longer. He lunged toward her. "Look what you did, you little—"

"No, Johnny!" Jack yanked him back. Before Johnny could shake him off, Jack hollered to Andi, "You better get out of here."

Andi gave Jack a withering look. "You're as disgusting as Johnny for letting him treat me like that. You could have stepped in."

"How was I supposed to know he'd do such a—"

"You *should* have known!" Blinking back hot tears, Andi stormed out of the alley and onto the wooden sidewalk in a mixture of rage and shame.

"*¿Qué te pasa?*" Rosa demanded, running to catch up. She reached out and pulled Andi to a stop. "What is the matter with you?"

"Oh, Rosa!" She would not cry. She *couldn't*. Not on the public street. She leaned against a lamppost and trembled while she described her encounter with Johnny. "How will I ever live through the school term? Johnny will happily shoot his mouth off to shame me even more. I'll be the laughingstock of the classroom." She shuddered. "Kissed by Johnny Wilson. What could be worse than that?"

"Maybe he will keep quiet for fear of your brothers," Rosa said.

As usual, Andi's Mexican friend was talking sense. The Carter brothers could make life miserable for Johnny Wilson if they found out what he'd been up to. But it meant she would have to tell them. She couldn't. It was too humiliating. She shook her head. "Johnny has nothing to fear from my brothers. I don't plan on telling them."

"Is that wise?"

"I don't care if it's wise or not. I'm not telling *anybody*. And you can't either. The sooner we forget about this, the better."

Andi pushed away from the lamppost and untied Taffy from the hitching rail. She might be able to forget about Johnny, but what about Jack? He'd seen the whole thing.

She was furious with Jack—partly because he hadn't stood up for her, and partly because he was stupid to get tangled up with Johnny. She yanked Taffy's reins from the rail. How could she work at Goodwin's alongside Jack *now*? He was acting just like Johnny. He would never let Andi forget what happened today.

I'll have to put up with his smirking face every day. She sighed. *Is Mother's gift worth all this?*

"Good morning, ladies. What brings you to town?"

Andi jumped. Justin was strolling up the boardwalk. He smiled and waved a greeting. Andi groaned inwardly. *Not now!*

"Remember," she whispered to Rosa from the side of her mouth, "not a word." Then she forced a smile. "Howdy, Justin. Rosa and I had . . . I mean *I* had some extra money and thought I'd"— she exchanged a meaningful glance with Rosa—"look around Goodwin's to see what there is to see . . ." Her voice trailed away at the knowing look on Justin's face.

"So, Chad paid you after all."

Andi nodded, annoyed. That Chad! He wasn't going to wire Mother about what had happened in the orchard, but it looked like he'd blabbed to Justin. Mitch and Melinda probably knew by now too. She was sure glad she hadn't told Chad the reason she needed money. He couldn't keep his mouth shut.

"Have you eaten?" Justin smoothly changed the subject. "I'm heading down to the Sequoia for an early lunch. Would you ladies care to join me?"

Andi's relief was genuine. "You bet, big brother. I'm starved." She retied Taffy to the railing and fell into step beside Justin. Maybe food and drink would erase the sickening memory of her recent encounter with Johnny Wilson.

Chapter Six

A JOB FOR ANDI

A ndi headed to Goodwin's Mercantile right after school the
following Monday. She arrived breathless, much to the shopkeeper's obvious amusement. "You needn't be in such a hurry," he
said. "The work won't disappear. How was your first day of school?"

"Like any other school day," Andi replied with a shrug. "Long."

Mr. Goodwin chuckled and led Andi to a counter of yard goods.
"Since Mrs. Goodwin passed away, the store has sorely lacked a fem-
inine touch. Your job will be to keep the shelves stocked and neat,
and to make them appealing to the customers. My wife really knew
how to make things look homey. I'm afraid I just don't have the
touch."

"I'll do the best I can," Andi promised. She surveyed the store
with a critical eye. Her gaze fell on the bolts of fabric scattered hap-
hazardly on the counter. "If I could use some of those shelves along
the wall"—she pointed behind the counter—"I could arrange the
bolts and stack them up. They would be at eye level so people could
see them better."

"You go right ahead and work on it," came Mr. Goodwin's relieved
reply. "When you're finished, I want you to straighten up by the cash
register. The customers have no place to lay their purchases." He
smiled. "I'll be in the stockroom unpacking merchandise. If someone comes in, give me a holler."

Andi nodded and helped herself to a large white apron hanging from a nearby peg. She tied it around her dress and made her way to the shelves. "This job is going to be fun," she told herself when Mr. Goodwin had disappeared into the back room. "Better than picking peaches, and *much* better than mucking out stalls."

An hour later, Andi backed up to examine her work. She nodded in satisfaction. "It doesn't look half bad." Each bolt of fabric was clearly visible, and the rainbow of colors blended together to give one wall of the store a cheerful, welcoming look.

"You're right," a quiet voice agreed.

Andi looked around. Mr. Goodwin stood in the stockroom doorway with his arms crossed.

He smiled at her. "Nicely done. The counters are clean, you refilled the candy jars, and you swept up the cracker crumbs around the barrel. You've managed to accomplish quite a bit in an hour."

"I enjoyed it," Andi replied. "I wish straightening my room was this much fun."

"I think you and I are going to get along fine. Your hour is about up. Sweep the walk for me before you go. If Jack comes in"— Mr. Goodwin's expression turned grim—"tell him there's plenty of work for him in the back."

Andi took the broom. The hour had flown by! She started for the door, but paused to glance at the window display, where her mother's gift lay. She leaned the broom against the wall and picked up the music box. Lifting the lid, she listened to it play a few bars of the lullaby. She closed her eyes and tried to imagine the look on her mother's face when she opened her gift.

"A few weeks and you'll be mine," she whispered, closing the lid with a sigh. "I'll wrap you in the prettiest paper I can find and—"

"What're you doing?"

Andi clutched the music box to her chest and spun around. Jack Goodwin stood next to the open doorway, watching her. His dark hair was tousled and his clothes unkempt. A piece of licorice hung from his mouth. He bit off a generous hunk and started chewing. With his free hand, he snatched the music box from Andi's hands and plunked it down in the window display.

"You weren't thinking about stealing this, were you?"

Andi flinched as if slapped. A hot rush of color flooded her cheeks. How dare Jack accuse her of stealing!

Jack glanced from the music box to Andi's red face. "I betcha you *were* stealing. Wouldn't that make a swell headline for the *Expositor*? 'Carter Girl Caught Stealing.' Maybe I'll get the sheriff."

"Don't be ridiculous," Andi snapped, finding her voice at last. She reached for the broom. "I was doing no such thing."

"So you say." Jack's eyes narrowed. "Hey! What are you doing with our broom?"

"I'm sweeping the walk." She shoved past Jack and went outside.

Jack followed. "Why?"

"Because your father hired me."

"He *what*?"

"I asked for a job and he gave me one." Andi ran the broom up and down the wooden sidewalk in front of the mercantile then returned to the store.

"Why do you need a job? Your family's rich." Jack swallowed his licorice and waited for an answer.

Andi stood the broom against the wall and faced Jack. He was a nice-looking boy, with his dark hair and bright, hazel eyes. It was too bad Johnny had a grip on him. "Well, Jack," she finally said, "I'll tell you why I have a job if you'll tell me why you're going around with Johnny. You've changed, and I don't like it. It's hard to believe we used to be friends."

Jack glared at her. "Johnny's right. You *are* too high and mighty. I don't care if you like it or not. I don't need your help choosing my friends."

"Some friend." She untied the apron from her waist and hung it up. "You'll end up in jail—or worse—with Johnny as your friend."

"Get out of here, Andi! Get out before I forget you're a girl and I throw you out."

"You'll do nothing of the kind, boy." Mr. Goodwin slapped his hand down on the counter then pointed to the stockroom. "You get back there and stock these shelves. Leave my new help alone."

"New help?" Jack sneered. He made no move to obey his father. "I won't work with her, Pa."

Mr. Goodwin made his way around the counter and grasped Jack's arm. "If you keep coming home this late every day, son, you won't have to worry about working *with* her. She'll do it all herself." He gave Jack a yank and said, "Good-bye, Andi. See you tomorrow."

Andi leaned over the counter and watched Mr. Goodwin scribble her first week's wages down on the tally sheet, right beneath the eight dollars she already had on account. "You're a good worker, Andi. Keep it up, and you'll have that music box paid off in no time." He folded the paper and slipped it into the cash register for safekeeping.

"I'm counting on it, sir, but . . ." She paused, uncertain how to bring up a thought that had been nagging her all week.

Mr. Goodwin frowned. "But what? Speak up."

"What if . . . I mean, I saw . . . that is, I'm not the only one interested in the music box," she said in a rush. "Three others were looking at it this week. I heard Mrs. King gushing over it and—"

Mr. Goodwin broke into a hearty laugh. "Don't worry, Andi. That music box is yours. If anyone else wants one, they'll have to place an order and wait their turn."

"Really?" Relief flooded her. Mr. Goodwin was kind.

"Your mother's a lucky woman," he said with a wistful smile. "She's certainly going to be surprised."

"So long as she doesn't walk in one afternoon when I'm working."

Andi hoped that didn't happen. How would she ever explain? "My real worry is that Justin will finish up the big legal case he's working on before I've paid off the music box. Then how would I wrangle an extra hour in town every day?" She headed for the door.

"Oh, Andi," Mr. Goodwin called her back. "Next Friday I'll be in San Francisco on a buying trip. The store will be closed, so you needn't come by."

"All right." She slumped inwardly. That meant one day's less wages.

"I was wondering if you could come by on Saturday instead."

Andi brightened. "Sure!"

"You and Jack can give me a hand unloading and stocking the shelves."

"You know Jack doesn't like working with me," Andi replied. "He grumbles and complains the days we're together."

"Don't pay any attention to his griping, Andi. Haven't you noticed that all of a sudden he's been coming home on time?" His lip twitched. "I threatened to give you his pay if he didn't start earning it."

"Really?" Would Mr. Goodwin make good his threat? It would certainly be a quick way to earn the rest of the money. Mother's birthday was fast approaching. "I'll try to come by next Saturday. What time?"

"I'll catch the early train back to Fresno, so how about mid afternoon?"

Andi thought a moment. Riding into town alone was out of the question. Perhaps she could talk Rosa into coming along. Justin would no doubt be working, but she preferred not to ride with him. He might ask questions about her sudden interest in visiting Fresno.

"That will be fine," she said. "I'll see you on Saturday. Good-bye." She ignored Jack when he passed her on his way home from a delivery. Not even his surly frown could dim Andi's contentment this afternoon.

Rosa met her in front of Justin's office. "So, *amiga*, you have worked at the mercantile for one week. Perhaps you are now ready to give up this *loco* idea."

"You didn't think it was *loco* last week when I went in and asked for the job. In fact, if I remember right, getting a job in town was your idea."

Rosa rolled her eyes. "That was before this trouble with Johnny and Jack. Nothing good will come from standing up to such a bully. He stole a kiss. What will he steal next?"

"Rosa, you promised not to bring up that business with Johnny," Andi sharply reminded her friend. "Not a whisper of what happened has circulated around the schoolroom, which means Johnny is keeping his mouth shut."

She sighed in relief. Her humiliating encounter with Johnny Wilson the week before was now only a bitter memory. She hoped the memory would soon vanish like a puff of smoke from a dying fire.

When Johnny had simmered down he probably realized what a fool he'd been. Bragging about it would only lead to trouble with the Carter family. The young man was a hothead, but he wasn't stupid.

"I am happy for you," Rosa said, "and I have told no one about your job. You are right. I am silly to worry about such a small matter. This business will soon be finished, and your mother will have the most beautiful music box in the valley."

Andi agreed. "Buying my mother this gift is important to me, Rosa. I'm going to stick with it until I earn that music box, in spite of Jack or Johnny or *anybody*." She squeezed her friend's hand. "Thanks for keeping my secret."

"Ready to go, ladies?" Justin stepped from his office.

Once settled in the buggy, Andi relaxed and leaned back to enjoy the hour-long ride out to the ranch. She smiled to herself. For once in her life, one of her ideas was working. In spite of her failure in the orchard, it now looked like she'd earn her mother's gift in plenty of time.

She closed her eyes and softly hummed "Brahms' Lullaby." *Everything's working perfectly at last. Nothing can go wrong—nothing at all.*

Chapter Seven

WRONG PLACE, WRONG TIME

Justin!" Andi tore into her brother's law office the following Friday and slammed the door behind her. The smell of rich leather and old cigars met her, along with the irritated voice of her brother's clerical assistant.

"What do you want, Miss Carter?"

Andi grinned at Tim O'Neil. "I want to see Justin, of course. Why else would I be yelling for him?"

"One does not enter the office of a respected lawyer in the same manner as one enters a cook shack or a saloon. What if he were in conference with a client?"

Andi laughed. Tim always acted stuffy toward her. Did he think he worked in San Francisco for some highbrow lawyer? "If he were with a client," she said, "you wouldn't be talking this nicely to me."

She sailed past Tim's desk and rapped on the door to her brother's private office.

"Come in."

Andi strolled into the office. "Are you ready to go? It's a beautiful day, and Rosa and I want to go home. I haven't ridden Taffy in days."

Justin looked up. "Sorry, Andi. I was tied up in court all morning, and it put me further behind than usual." He tapped the stack of books and documents piled high on his desk. "It'll be awhile." He frowned. "Why are you in such an all-fired hurry this afternoon? Most days I don't see you for another hour."

Oops!

It was time to make a quick exit, before Justin asked her what she'd been doing with her extra time all week. She backed up toward the door. "Maybe Rosa and I will wander over to La Casita and see if we can catch a ride back to the ranch. Diego or José might be there."

"The *cantina* is clear across town."

"We haven't anything else to do," Andi said. "If we find a ride, I'll come by and let you know. Please? I really want to go riding this afternoon."

"Fine"—Justin mumbled his permission and picked up a pen— "but don't forget to tell me if you leave town. I don't want to spend the evening looking for you."

Andi left the office and joined Rosa on the boardwalk. "Justin's busy, but I got permission to try to find us a ride home. Perhaps your father's in town. Let's check the *cantina*."

Rosa agreed wholeheartedly. They hurried down Tulare Street until they reached the railroad tracks. The depot was mostly deserted, and the next train wasn't due until that evening.

Andi waved to Mr. Owens, the telegrapher, and crossed the tracks to the west side of town. "Let's take a shortcut through the ware-house district," she suggested. "Then we won't have to walk so far."

Rosa sighed. "I do not like your shortcuts, Andi. Last time, we ended up past G Street, which was *muy lejos*—very far—from where we wanted to be." She shivered, although the sun was hot. "All kinds of drifters and bad *hombres* hang around the warehouse district."

"They hang around the stockyards," Andi corrected, "and we're not going that way."

Rosa shrugged her acceptance and followed Andi into a side street between Noble Brothers Packing & Storage and Jake's Pawn Shop. They threaded their way among workers hurrying to keep up with a harvest in full swing. The sweet smell of ripe peaches filled the air.

The streets became less crowded after the girls scurried past the packinghouse. Soon they were alone, surrounded by dark, quiet buildings, many with cracked or missing window panes. They skirted around broken glass and the rusting remains of farm equipment.

"If this is a shorter way to the Mexican part of town, why does no one else use it?" Rosa glanced at the gloomy shadows and piles of debris. "I think maybe because it is *not* so short," she answered her own question.

"Shh!" Andi laid a hand on Rosa's arm and stopped. "Did you hear that?"

"Hear what?"

"It sounds like whimpering or crying or something. Listen!" Andi held up her hand. "There it is again."

Rosa caught her breath. "*Sí.* I hear it. An animal of some kind. Perhaps a mad dog. We should leave."

"It doesn't sound like a mad dog," Andi scoffed. "It sounds like a puppy whining. Come on. Let's go see."

"No," Rosa said. "You are *loco.* I am not going down that alley. Neither should you. Remember the last alley you rushed into."

"It'll only take a minute," Andi argued. "I doubt Johnny Wilson is waiting for me with a crying pup."

Rosa stood her ground. "If you wish to go, I cannot stop you. But I will stay here. There must be one of us left alive to tell *Señor* Justin."

"Tell him what?" Andi asked, exasperated. "There's nothing to tell."

"Good. Then I will stay here and tell nothing."

Andi took off down the darkened alleyway. She quickened her pace when she heard a loud yelp and more whining. A minute later, she came face-to-face with the source of the desperate noises.

"Oh, you poor thing!" Andi exclaimed. She turned and called to Rosa in a loud voice. "I found the puppy!"

Rosa's answer came back as a distant echo. "Good. Hurry back!"

A stone's throw away, a small, black pup was limping—obviously in pain. Each time he put weight on his front paw, he whined and stumbled another step.

Andi didn't intend to dawdle, not in this dark alley. She leaped forward to gather the little animal in her arms, but the puppy had other plans. With a yelp, he hobbled into the space between two crates and turned a circle to stare at the strange girl.

"Come here, little fella. I won't hurt you," Andi coaxed in a quiet and soothing tone. "Let me see what's wrong." She slowly crept toward the injured dog.

The puppy regarded Andi for a moment, then backed up before she could grab him. He turned tail and limped away.

"I only want to help you." Andi chased the dog deeper into the twists and turns of the warehouse district's back streets. Then she stopped and glanced around. It was quiet. *Too* quiet. Even the puppy had stopped crying.

"How far have I come?" The whole area looked deserted, and more run-down than before. "Rosa!" Her voice echoed in the shadows. "Can you hear me?"

"*Sí,*" came her friend's faint reply.

Heartened by the sound of Rosa's voice, Andi turned back to the puppy. "I'm giving you one last chance. If you don't let me help you, I'm going back. I don't scare easy, but this place makes my skin crawl."

The dog answered with a whimper and started chewing on his paw.

Andi took advantage of the distraction and lunged, catching the puppy by his back foot. He yipped and strained to free himself. For a moment she thought the dog might bite her, but he seemed intent only on getting away.

Andi hung on. "Will . . . you . . . stop . . . struggling!" She settled herself to the ground and dragged the hurt puppy into her lap. She gently lifted the paw and winced. A large thorn was imbedded between his toes.

"Oh, you poor thing. That looks nasty." She steadied her fingers and grasped the thorn. With one quick yank, she pulled the thorn out and cast it aside. Blood and pus spilled from the wound. Andi made a face. "Well, little fella, I bet you start feeling better in no time."

The dog stopped crying and began to lick his paw. Then he looked up and wagged his tail. When Andi patted his head, the puppy pushed his cold, wet nose into her hand and licked it.

Andi scratched behind his long, floppy ears. "You're adorable. I'm going to ask Mother if I can keep you." She could think of no reason why she wouldn't be allowed to keep the pup. There was always room on a large ranch for another dog.

She stood up and cuddled him in her arms. "If Mother says no," she decided, laying her cheek next to his soft fur, "one of the ranch hands will take you."

Crash! A door's loud slam and an angry shout from somewhere overhead jerked Andi from her pleasant thoughts. The reality of where she was hit home. She had recklessly followed a dog down a little-used alley and into a part of town she'd never visited.

Rosa was right. *I should have listened to her.* Who knew what kind of people wandered these back streets?

Andi flashed a startled glance upward. Across the alley, two dark figures struggled together at the top of the stairs to an old, ramshackle building. Andi didn't know if it was a warehouse or a boarding house or *what* kind of place it was. Nor did she care. The cursing, the yelling, and the sound of blows reminded her that she was in the wrong part of town.

Andi clutched the puppy and flattened herself against the side of the building. *I have to get out of here!* Her heart beat wildly. She closed her eyes and took a deep breath. *Please, God. I'm sorry I came this way. I don't want to be seen. Please show me the way out. I'm so turned around.*

"No more!" A man's frantic voice sliced through Andi's hasty prayer. "You hear me? Not a penny more!"

The words sent a shiver of fear down Andi's spine. She opened her eyes and peeked around the corner. The alley was narrow, and the stairway's landing stood just across from where she hid. No matter which direction she fled, she'd have to pass right by it to gain her freedom.

She looked up. At the top of the stairs the men continued to punch each other. They hadn't even glanced Andi's way.

The buildings cast long shadows from the late afternoon sun, throwing the alley into gloom. Perhaps if she hurried, she could slip by unnoticed. She didn't care if her escape took her deeper into the alleys or back toward the main street. Either way, she'd be away from the two men. She tightened her hold on the wriggling dog and stepped out from her hiding place.

"Let go of me!"

Andi froze. She watched in horror as the smaller of the two men accompanied his yell with a last, desperate shove. The larger, heavier man gave a half-choked cry and pitched backward, help-lessly flailing his arms. He bounced down the long flight of steps then crashed through the handrail halfway down. He dropped like a stone and landed with a final *crunch* less than a dozen feet from Andi.

The man on the landing appeared not to notice Andi. His atten-tion was riveted on the still form lying on the ground. "Oh no! Please, God, no!" A wrenching sob came from his throat. He clat-tered down the steps and fell to his knees beside the man. "What have I done?" He bowed his head and sobbed. "Oh, God, forgive me. I didn't mean to—"

The puppy whined.

With a start, the man leaped to his feet. His eyes widened when he saw Andi. They locked gazes for half a second. Then without a word or a backward glance, the man flew past Andi and disappeared into the shadows.

The puppy yelped and struggled to free himself. Andi ignored the

ANDREA CARTER AND THE PRICE OF TRUTH

yapping. She stood rooted in shock, staring at what appeared to be a very dead man.

When the puppy's claw scratched her arm, Andi came to herself. She relaxed her crushing grip and forced her gaze away from the still form on the ground. Her heart raced. She didn't know the large man lying dead in front of her, but she knew something worse.

She knew the killer.

Chapter Eight

JUSTIN STEPS IN

Hugging the dog tightly to her chest, Andi gave the dead man a wide berth and dashed away in the opposite direction of the killer. *I've got to find Justin.* She didn't know what else to do. *He'll never believe who I saw.*

What would Justin say when she told him what happened? She had a hard time believing it herself. Panting, she raced around another building and headed for the light. A few minutes later, she emerged from the alley.

Andi didn't stop running until she spotted her friend. The puppy hung from one arm, his legs swinging.

"So, you found the *perrito*," Rosa said. "Will you keep him? Was he—"

"Let's get out of here!" Andi cut her off. "Hurry!"

"You are frightened," Rosa observed with a pleased nod. "That is good. Now perhaps there will be no more—how do you say it—shortcuts?"

Andi grabbed Rosa with her free hand. "Come *on!*" She lifted the puppy higher and gave Rosa a tug to hurry her along. When they reached the railroad tracks, she slowed down. "You've . . . got to . . . get Sheriff Tate," she said between gasps.

"The sheriff? *¿Por qué?*"

"Because . . ." Andi took another gulp of air. Slowly, her beating heart returned to normal. "You've got to take him back to the alley. There's a man lying there either unconscious or dead." She swallowed. "I think he's dead."

Rosa gasped.

"Do it," Andi pleaded, giving her friend a shake. She thrust the black puppy into Rosa's arms. "Take care of him. I'll explain everything later. I've got to find Justin."

Trusting Rosa to do as she asked, Andi took off down Tulare Street. By the time she stumbled onto the boardwalk in front of her brother's office, she was out of breath and shaking. She wasn't crying—yet—but her tears were close to the surface. Without pausing to collect her thoughts, she crashed through the door. "Justin!"

Tim jumped up at her appearance. Papers flew from his hand. "Miss Carter, I insist you enter this office in a way that does not embarrass your brother or distress his clients." He pointed to a chair. "Sit down."

Andi shot past the annoyed clerk without so much as an apology.

Tim scurried around his desk and planted himself in front of Justin's private office. "You can't go in there. Mr. Carter told me that not even the governor himself was to be admitted—not until he finished his work. You've already disrupted him once this afternoon."

Tears welled up in Andi's eyes, but she blinked them back. "Let me see my brother," she demanded between clenched teeth.

Tim crossed his arms over his chest. "No."

"Justin," Andi shouted through the closed door, "I need to talk to you!"

The door opened and Justin appeared. He looked irritated. "Young lady, you are sorely trying my patience this afternoon. I have a clerk for a reason. Would you please try to respect that?"

Andi elbowed her way past Tim. "Oh, Justin!" She threw her arms around his waist and buried her head against his strong chest. "You've got to tell me what to do." She burst into tears.

"What on earth?"

56

"I'm sorry, Mr. Carter," Tim said. "I tried to keep her out."

"Never mind. I'll take care of this."

He drew Andi into his office, closed the door, and led her across the room. "What's the matter, honey?" he asked softly as he untangled her arms from around his waist. Concern replaced his irritated expression. He lowered her into his chair and perched himself on the edge of his desk. "Now settle down and tell me what's wrong."

Andi swallowed her sobs and looked up. "He killed him, Justin. I saw him."

"*What?* Who?" Justin demanded. "Who killed whom? Where?"

"In an alley. It all happened so fast. I was so scared." She quickly related the details of the fight and ended with, "When Peter ran away, I ran too."

Justin's astonished look bored into her. "Peter? Peter *Wilson*? Are you certain?"

Andi nodded. "I saw him, Justin. The other man *might* be unconscious, but I think . . . I think he's dead." She rubbed her watery eyes. "What should I do?"

Justin reached into his pocket and pulled out a large white handkerchief. "First of all, wipe your eyes and blow your nose. Then"—he slid from his perch and straightened up—"we find the sheriff."

Sheriff Tate wasn't in his office, which didn't surprise Andi. "He probably went to see what happened. I sent Rosa for him."

Sure enough, when Justin and Andi reached the alley, Sheriff Tate and Rosa, along with a couple of deputies, were standing around, staring grim-faced at the dead man.

The sheriff called Justin over. "Glad to see you, Justin. Rosa Garduño burst into my office a bit ago and dragged me over here." He looked at Rosa, who stood next to Deputy Hayes and still clutched the wiggly pup. "She told me your sister sent her."

Andi jumped down from the buggy and ran to her friend. Rosa immediately plopped the dog into Andi's outstretched hands.

"That's right, Russ." Justin glanced down. "It's Ben Decker."

Sheriff Tate nodded. "Looks like he finally got what was comin' to him. Once too often in the bottle, I'd say. Must've slipped on the steps and taken his final tumble." He rubbed his whiskered chin and looked thoughtfully at the still form. "I can't figure out what he was doing up in that old warehouse, though. He usually finds a dark, quiet corner to do his drinkin' in." He sighed. "Did you two girls just stumble across this poor fellow?"

Rosa burst into frantic Spanish. *"¡No, señor! ¡Yo no! ¡No sé nada! Andi me dijo que—"*

"Take it easy," the sheriff said, holding up a hand. "It doesn't matter." He glanced at Justin. "The coroner will schedule an inquest, of course, but it looks like an accident to me. Doesn't surprise me none," he added.

Justin laid a hand on the sheriff's shoulder. "Russ . . ." He paused, clearly unhappy at what he was about to say. "Andi saw what happened."

Sheriff Tate shot a stern look at Andi. "That so?"

Andi nodded.

"Well, girl, don't leave me guessing. What happened?"

"They were fighting," Andi said in a small voice, "and—"

"Who?" Sheriff Tate demanded.

Andi swallowed. "P-Peter. Peter Wilson."

"Peter Wilson!" the sheriff burst out. "I don't believe it."

"You'd better believe it, Russ," Justin said, "because now you've got a witness."

Chapter Nine

AN UNLIKELY SUSPECT

Justin pulled the buggy to a stop in front of a large, stately mansion on the edge of town.

Sheriff Tate dismounted and tied his horse to the ornate hitching post. He strolled over to the buggy and sighed. "Are you absolutely sure about this?" He aimed his question at Andi.

Andi twisted the handkerchief she held in her lap. "Yes, sir."

How many times had the sheriff asked her that? She wished Rosa was here, but Deputy Hayes had escorted her back to the ranch. Andi didn't even have her new puppy for comfort. Justin had sent the animal home with Rosa.

Sheriff Tate stepped aside as Justin climbed down from the rig. "I have to knock on that door"—he pointed at the house—"and take the Wilson boy in for questioning. I don't want to do it, Justin. What if Peter really is innocent? No one will believe he's guilty. I don't believe it myself. This could get ugly."

"I know." Justin helped Andi from the buggy. "But I'm afraid you have no choice. Andi says she saw him. If Peter's smart, he'll admit to the killing and let Andi testify about the fight. A plea of self-defense could save him a lot of misery."

Sheriff Tate didn't agree. "I hope you know what you're getting us all into, young lady. Even if it *was* an accident, I sure wouldn't want to cross Charles Wilson. He thinks the world of Peter."

"You're not helping matters, Russ," Justin said.

The sheriff grunted and led the way through the gate and up the walk.

Andi hung back. "Do I have to do this?"

Justin held the gate open and motioned Andi through. "You've got to face him sooner or later."

A cobblestone walkway wound its way through an eye-catching, well-watered garden—the showcase of uptown Fresno and the pride of Alice Wilson. Climbing roses in full bloom encircled the four white columns of the wide porch. An alabaster birdbath stood near the steps.

Sheriff Tate climbed the steps and grasped the large, lion's head knocker, giving it three loud thuds against the door. Andi cringed at each knock.

The Wilsons' Chinese house-servant, Li, answered. "Good evening, Sheriff." If he was surprised at these unexpected suppertime visitors, he gave no sign. He bowed and led them into the wide foyer. "Please wait here." He slipped away.

A smiling Charles Wilson joined them a few minutes later. Andi knew his delight at seeing the visitors was genuine. Except for her little misunderstanding at the bank a couple of weeks ago, the bank president was cheerful and always spoke kindly to her. He greeted his guests with a hearty handshake and an invitation to supper. "Can you stay? I'll tell Alice to put on—"

"Charles . . ." the sheriff began uneasily, clutching his hat.

Mr. Wilson looked around at the grim faces. When his gaze fell on Andi, his smile faded. "I guess this isn't a social call, after all. What has Jonathan done *now*?" He seemed completely aware of his younger son's reputation as a troublemaker. "Whatever it is, I promise I'll straighten it out." He nodded at his servant. "Li, find Jonathan and ask him to join us."

Li moved to obey, but the sheriff held him back. "We're not here about Jonathan."

AN UNLIKELY SUSPECT

"Really?" Mr. Wilson shoved his spectacles higher on his nose and chuckled. "That's the best news I've had all day."

"Is Peter home?" Sheriff Tate asked.

"Of course. He's upstairs, packing for a trip to Yosemite that he and Mitch planned. I gave him a few days off. Wouldn't want it said that I worked the lad to death."

"May we speak with him?" Justin asked.

Mr. Wilson frowned. "Is this an official visit, Sheriff?"

The sheriff shuffled uncomfortably. "I'm afraid so. Ben Decker was found dead in an alley over in the warehouse district. Peter was seen scuffling with him moments before his death."

Mr. Wilson stiffened. "Peter? In the company of that drunk? Impossible." He narrowed his eyes. "I resent what you're implying."

"I'm sorry, Charles," the sheriff said. "I find it incredibly hard to believe too. However"—he cleared his throat and nervously fingered his hat—"there's an eyewitness."

Mr. Wilson's eyebrows shot up. "An eyewitness from the warehouse district? I'm surprised at you, Russ. You'd actually believe a witness from that part of town? It's obvious someone is playing a cruel joke on us all—slandering my son's good name. I'll put a stop to that quickly enough. Who is this eyewitness?"

"You're not making this any easier," Sheriff Tate said. "Andi saw the whole thing."

The banker gaped at her. His spectacles slid down his nose.

Andi wanted to hide behind Justin, but she forced her feet to stay put.

"Go get Peter," Mr. Wilson snapped at his servant. "Let's hear what he has to say."

Li bowed and left to summon his employer's son.

Andi felt sweat trickle under her dress collar. She wiped her clammy hands against her skirt. Would Peter tell the truth? She shuddered, suddenly cold. *What if he doesn't? Will anyone believe what I saw? Lord, please help me get through this.*

A few minutes later, Peter appeared at the top of the wide stair-case. He was dressed in denim britches, a heavy cotton shirt, and a vest. He slung a set of saddlebags and a jacket over his shoulder and descended the stairs two at a time. He shook hands with the adults and grinned at Andi. "Hi, Andi."

Andi started. How could Peter greet her so casually? Didn't he know why she was here? He *must* know. Yet he acted as if seeing the sheriff in his home was the most natural thing in the world. He was either a good actor or—Andi swallowed—he really *was* innocent. But that would mean—

No! It was Peter I saw. I'm sure of it.

Peter was talking. "Li said you wanted to see me, Father. I hope it won't take long. Mitch and I want to eat and be on our way." He glanced up the stairs at the tall, sandy-haired young man who appeared at the banister. "Yosemite, here we come! Right, Mitch?"

Mitch echoed Peter's enthusiasm. "You bet!" He gave his brother and sister a careless wave. "Howdy, Sis. Hi, Justin. What're you two doing here?" He hurried down the stairs.

"They're not here for supper," Mr. Wilson said tightly. He glared at Andi. She drew back from the banker's hostile gaze and pressed closer to Justin.

Peter set his jacket and saddlebags aside and faced the sheriff. "So, what's going on?"

"Ben Decker has been found dead in an alley," Sheriff Tate said. "It happened about an hour ago."

Peter's eyes widened. "Ben Decker? Really? That's too bad, but I doubt many folks will mourn the old drunk's passing." He frowned. "Why are you telling me this?"

"Have you seen Ben today?"

Peter snorted. "No, Sheriff, I have not. Besides the fact that Ben Decker and I don't travel in the same circles, I was at the bank most of the day." He glanced from the sheriff to Justin. "What's all this about, Justin?"

"You were seen involved in a scuffle with Ben that led to his death," Sheriff Tate explained before Justin could speak.

"I haven't been anywhere near Ben," Peter insisted.

Mr. Wilson let out a relieved breath. "That should clear things up for you, Russ."

Sheriff Tate ignored the banker. "Is this the man you saw this afternoon, Andi?"

She nodded miserably.

"Wait a minute," Mitch broke in. "There must be some kind of mistake. Peter was at the bank all morning, and I was with him this afternoon. We were planning our trek to Yosemite."

Justin whirled on his brother. "You were with him *all* afternoon?"

Mitch bristled. "Don't cross-examine me, Justin."

"Can you vouch for Peter's whereabouts between four and five this evening?" Sheriff Tate's question sounded official.

"I reckon not for every minute. We split up for a while." Mitch shrugged. "So what? Peter would never kill anyone—intentionally or by accident." He turned to Andi. "You must have seen somebody else."

Andi stared at Mitch in astonishment. Did he really believe that?

Justin gave Mitch a warning look and focused on Andi. "Are you *certain* this is the man you saw fighting with Ben Decker?"

Andi's throat tightened until she could barely get the words out. "Yes, Justin. I'm sure."

"I'm sorry, Charles," the sheriff said. "I hope you understand my part in this. I've got a witness who says she saw Peter cause the death of Ben Decker. I have to take him in. The inquest is tomorrow morning, and—"

"*What?*" The blood drained from the banker's face. "This is absurd. Peter hasn't even *seen* Ben. Doesn't his word count for anything?"

Peter glanced at Andi. For the first time that evening he looked uneasy. "It must be an honest mistake," he said, echoing Mitch's reaction. "Those alleys are mighty dark back there. Maybe you saw somebody who looked like me?" His look turned pleading.

Andi didn't answer. She felt sick seeing Peter look so . . . so desperate.

Justin faced Mr. Wilson and his son. When he spoke, Andi recognized his lawyer voice—strong and no-nonsense. "I want you to know how terrible I feel. The last thing I want is for this to go to trial. It would be better all around, Peter, if you came clean about what happened. From what Andi told me, it sounds like a fair fight that ended with a tragic accident. You have an excellent chance of clearing your name and going free. Let's end this right now and save both our families from having to go on public display."

Peter shook his head. "I haven't done anything wrong. Furthermore, I don't want my family's name mentioned in the same breath as that no-account, drunken fool, Ben Decker." He crossed the room and searched Andi's face. "Why are you doing this, Andi? Our families have known each other since before you were born. Mitch and I are best friends."

A huge lump rose to Andi's throat. Why was Peter lying? They had looked into each other's eyes that dreadful moment before he ran away. He *knew* he was guilty.

Peter took her gently by the shoulders. "Please admit it was a mistake. It must have been dark. You saw a quick glimpse of a running man and mistook him for me. That's the only reasonable explanation." His grip tightened. "What does it matter, anyway? Don't you understand? Nobody cares that he's dead."

Andi pulled away from Peter and backed into Justin, who put an arm around her. "God cares," she whispered past her tight throat.

Peter seemed taken aback by her answer. He looked helplessly at his father.

Mr. Wilson's face was a mask of stone. "All right, if that's the way you want it. I'll get the best lawyer in the state. We'll get to the bottom of this foolishness if it's the last—"

"That's enough, Charles." Sheriff Tate looked from Mr. Wilson to Peter to Andi. "Justin, you'd better take Andi home."

Justin nodded and turned to Mitch. "It's probably a good idea if you head back to the ranch too."

Mitch let out a heavy sigh. "Yeah, I reckon." He scowled at his sister. "I guess I won't be enjoying a trip to Yosemite before roundup, after all." He headed upstairs to collect his things.

Andi left the Wilson home with a headache and a heavy heart. She climbed into the buggy, clasped her hands tightly in her lap, and stared straight ahead.

Justin slapped the reins. "I'm sorry you had to be there. I know it wasn't pleasant."

"Do I have to go to the inquest tomorrow?"

"Yes, but don't worry. An inquest is not a trial. It only determines how Ben Decker died and if there was foul play involved."

"If I hadn't been in that alley, they'd probably decide it was an accident, right?"

Justin was silent.

"Isn't that right, Justin?"

He sighed. "Yes, but that's not the case. You *were* there. You have to tell what you saw. There will be a few questions and then it will be over."

Until the trial, Andi added, but she didn't say it aloud. Instead, she whispered, "I really hoped Peter would ask you to help him." She took a deep breath. "He means it, Justin. He's never going to admit he killed Mr. Decker. Maybe I'd better tell the sheriff I made a mistake."

"Have you made a mistake?"

"No. But nobody's going to believe me. Even Mitch thinks I'm wrong. My own brother."

"Mitch will come around." He found her cold hand and squeezed it. "Besides, it doesn't matter if anyone believes you or not. If you tell the truth, you have nothing to fear. You get up, say your piece, and sit down. That's all there is to it." He smiled at her.

Andi didn't smile back. She wasn't fooled one bit by her brother's words. She'd listened to him often enough to know when he sounded worried. He was worried now.

I should have let it go, she reflected. *Ben Decker is dead. Ruining Peter and hurting his family won't bring him back. Why did I ever open my mouth?*

Chapter Ten

AN UNWELCOME VISITOR

Andi ran the grooming brush along the smooth golden back of her palomino and sighed deeply. Spending time with Taffy usually pushed any gloomy thoughts to a little-used nook in her mind. Not today, though. Not even seeing Taffy's rounded belly and knowing she'd drop a foal in three short months cheered Andi this afternoon.

She dropped the brush onto the floor of Taffy's stall, offered the mare a few lumps of sugar, and said, "I've decided I don't care much for lawyers . . . or judges, for that matter. *Nobody* was smiling at the inquest this morning, not even Justin." She leaned against the stall door and allowed Taffy to nuzzle her, looking for more sugar.

After a few minutes of enjoying her friend's comical attempts to find a treat, Andi pulled the pockets of her overalls inside out. "It's all gone."

Taffy shook her mane and snorted.

"Is that all you ever think about? Treats?" Andi frowned.

Her scowl was not for Taffy's greed. The memory of the inquest buzzed inside her head like flies around the barnyard. "'Just get up, say your piece, and sit down.'" She mimicked her brother's words. "Sure. Easy as pie for a fancy, grown-up lawyer to say. *He* wasn't sitting up there while that pinched-face lawyer looked at me and clicked his tongue like I was a half-witted child."

She threw her arms around Taffy's neck. "He has shifty eyes too." She buried her face in her mare's creamy mane. "You should've seen all the people jammed inside the courthouse, like the inquest was the newest circus attraction. It made me—"

"Andi?"

Melinda's quiet voice brought Andi around with a start. Her sister was peering over the stall's half-door. The memory of the inquest faded. "Hi, Melinda."

"I see you wasted no time changing clothes and coming out here." She rested her arms on the door's ledge. "I hope you told Taffy how well you did at the inquest, and how proud we are of you."

Andi rubbed Taffy's nose. "Mitch isn't proud of me."

Melinda sighed. "Mitch just needs a little time. He and Peter have been friends since grammar school. You need to understand how upset he must be about all of this."

"No more upset than I am," Andi shot back. "Does Mitch think I'm lying?"

"Don't be silly. He only thinks you should consider the possibility that you might be mistaken."

Andi left her horse and joined Melinda at the door. "I *have* considered it—over and over—all night long and most of this morning." She shook her head. "It's no use. I saw him. Maybe only for a few seconds, but it was Peter."

"I believe you," Melinda said.

"Oh, Melinda, I hate this whole thing." Andi clenched a fist and slammed it against the wall. She knew proper young ladies did not hit things when they were frustrated, but right now she didn't feel much like a young lady. "I wish Peter would tell the truth and get it over with. Why won't he?" She searched Melinda's concerned blue eyes for an answer.

Melinda shrugged. "It makes no sense to me. Mother and Justin will be back from town soon. Maybe they can help." She glanced around the stall. "Are you going for a ride?"

"Yes. I want to keep Taffy in good shape as long as she feels up to it. She loves our rides as much as I do."

"Want some company?"

Andi looked away. "I'd rather go alone."

"I shouldn't leave you by yourself."

Andi turned back to Melinda in surprise. "I can take care of myself. There's nothing wrong with me that a good ride can't cure."

"All right," her sister reluctantly agreed. "If you're set on it."

"I am."

Melinda shrugged and left. She patted her horse Panda on the way out of the barn.

Andi lifted a bridle from a nearby hook. "Melinda doesn't know it," she said, placing the bit in Taffy's mouth and securing the headstall around her mare's head, "but the inquest is only one of my problems. The other problem is Mr. Goodwin."

Taffy stamped a foot.

"Yep. I was supposed to help him unpack today after his buying trip. I don't dare ride into town *now*, not with the way everyone is stirred up. I hope he understands." She smoothed out Taffy's creamy forelock, unlatched the stall door, and led her horse out of the barn.

In spite of the day's unpleasant beginning, Andi felt her spirits rise at the thought of a good, long ride on this beautiful September afternoon. She grabbed hold of Taffy's mane and was just about to scramble onto her bare back when the sight of a buggy rolling into the yard caught her attention.

A slender, clean-shaven man pulled the rig to a stop. "Good afternoon."

Andi loosened her hold on Taffy and faced the stranger. "Howdy."

The man climbed down from the buggy and walked toward her. He wore a pinstriped suit and shiny black shoes. A derby hat perched on his head. The words *city slicker* popped into Andi's head. She bit her lip to keep from giggling.

"Harvey Wellin, *San Francisco Chronicle*." He held out his hand. "This the Circle C ranch?"

A newspaper reporter. Andi no longer felt like laughing. "Yes, it is." She didn't shake his hand.

Mr. Wellin's hand fell to his side. He turned a full circle and slowly scanned the enormous, two-story Spanish *hacienda*, the lush green gardens and irrigated paddocks, and the numerous outbuildings. Then he whistled. "The Carters have quite a place here."

Andi didn't respond. She tightened her grip on Taffy's mane and willed the stranger to go away.

He didn't leave. Instead, he turned an annoying smile on Andi. "I'm looking for Andrea Carter."

"Why?" Her heart sank to her toes. She knew why.

Mr. Wellin wagged a finger in her face. "Now, darlin', that's no business of yours. You just run up to the house and fetch her for me."

Andi bristled. She didn't like being called *darling* by a rude stranger. She didn't like the way he was ordering her around. She also didn't like the fact he was a reporter.

Everything about Harvey Wellin reeked of bad manners and disrespect. "I think you'd better leave, before I call my brothers."

An empty threat. Chad and Mitch were out on the range and not due back until suppertime. But this nosy reporter didn't know that.

He chuckled. "You must be Andrea Carter." He whipped out a pad of paper and a pencil from an inside pocket of his suit coat. "I saw you from a distance this morning, but you looked . . . well . . . different." His gaze swept her overalls, plaid shirt, and wide-brimmed hat. His smile grew wider. "Never mind. Forgive my bad manners. I'd like to chat with you about the killing."

Andi winced at the word *killing*. She didn't want to talk about it. Not ever. Especially not to a big-city newspaper reporter, who would probably see to it that her story was plastered on the front page of every newspaper across central California. After all, the Wilsons were a respected and well-known family, as was—*unfortunately*, Andi thought—her own family. People dearly loved to read and gossip about rich folks' doings.

When Andi made no reply, Mr. Wellin frowned and inspected his pad. "I know there's a great story here. Back-alley murder—"

"Who said anything about murder?" Andi blurted. How did these stories grow into tall tales so quickly? It had only been one day.

Harvey licked the end of his pencil and winked at Andi. "Now we're getting somewhere, darlin'. I'll admit that murder may be too strong a word for what happened. Why don't you tell me *your* version of the events? I'm sure there's more to it than just the dry, hard facts that came out at the inquest."

Andi clamped her mouth shut, but the reporter kept talking. "I'm told Peter Wilson is an old and dear family friend." He took a step forward. "How do you feel about testifying against him? What does your brother Mitchell think about your testimony? There's a human-interest story here somewhere."

Andi backed against Taffy for support. Her heart fluttered.

"Do you know why Peter Wilson was fighting the town drunk in the first place? Did you hear what they were arguing about? Perhaps the drunk was blackmailing him. It sure wouldn't be the first time a rich man's son was involved in a scandal." He paused.

When Andi didn't answer, he frowned. "Give me *something*, Miss Carter. It's going to come out sooner or later. I'll be content with a quote or two from you. Then I'll be on my way."

Andi glanced around. Except for the steady clanging from the blacksmith's shop on the far side of the barn, the yard was quiet. Where was Sid, the foreman? Where was Diego? Where was *anybody*?

"What's the matter, darlin'? Cat got your tongue?"

Furious, Andi responded, but not in a way Mr. Harvey Wellin probably liked. "I won't tell you anything. I'm going riding." She snagged Taffy's mane and hoisted herself onto the palomino's back. *"Adiós."*

Mr. Wellin grabbed Taffy's bridle. "What's your hurry?"

71

Before Andi could react, the door to the ranch house opened. Melinda clattered down the porch steps and crossed the yard. A worried expression covered her face. "I thought you were going riding." She looked at the young man. "Who are you?"

"A nosy reporter from the city," Andi answered. "He wants to ask me a bunch of questions about yesterday."

"Let go of my sister's horse," Melinda said. When he obeyed, she smiled at him. "I'm sorry, sir, but Andi's not to talk to anyone about what happened yesterday. I'm afraid you'll have to leave." She took hold of Taffy's bridle and began to guide the pair toward one of the fenced paddocks.

"Wait a minute," Mr. Wellin burst out, running up behind them.

"Good day, sir," Melinda said, a hint of ice in her voice. "Or must I call our foreman to escort you off the ranch?" She nodded in the direction of the bunkhouse.

Sid McCoy had miraculously appeared on the porch and was leaning against a post. "Need some help, Miss Melinda?" he called.

The reporter flicked a nervous glance at the husky foreman, swallowed, and said to the girls, "It's been a pleasure, ladies." He touched the brim of his hat and took his leave.

Andi dissolved into laughter as the buggy disappeared down the road. "You sure put him in his place with your grand-lady airs, Melinda. Just like Mother. Thank you."

Melinda smiled. "I've had a lot of practice with my 'grand-lady' airs, as you call them. You should try it sometime instead of losing your temper and getting into quarrels." She shaded her eyes at the retreating buggy. "That's the last we'll see of him."

Andi lost her smile. "Maybe we won't see Mr. Wellin, but I bet there are plenty of others ready to take his place." She sighed. The encounter this afternoon was not the last of anything.

It was only the beginning.

Chapter Eleven

THE BULLY RETURNS

Mother insisted that Andi wait an entire week before going back to school, which suited Andi fine. She welcomed the chance to stay away from town. The week had been filled with words like *hearing, examination, evidence, district attorney, defense lawyer,* and *trial.*

Andi's thoughts were like tumbleweeds. She had to tell her story over and over. First to Matthew Powers, the prosecuting lawyer, who would try to prove Peter had killed Ben Decker. He was nice. Then to Maxwell Browning, Peter's defense lawyer—the shifty-eyed man from the inquest. He was *not* nice, but with Justin beside her on the settee, Mr. Browning at least kept his voice civil.

When it was decided that Peter would stand trial, the town buzzed with disapproval. People expected gunfighters and no-accounts to stand trial for killing good, innocent folks. They expressed outrage that a fine young man like Peter Wilson should go to court for *maybe* killing a worthless drunk.

It was into the middle of this hotbed of gossip that Andi returned to school the following Monday. She did not want to go. She didn't want to sit in class and feel the curious gazes of her schoolmates.

There would be questions, a *lot* of questions. The newspaper reporter had been persistent, but her friends would be worse. They'd pester her with questions, the girls shivering with gruesome delight at what Andi had been thrust into.

Justin broke into her thoughts. "Don't look so glum." He brought the buggy to a stop in front of the school and gave her braid an affectionate tug. "Things are moving pretty fast. This should all be over in a couple of weeks."

Andi's spirits drooped. Two more weeks. An eternity.

"Would you like me to take you back to the ranch?" Justin asked. "Mother warned you. Folks are stirred up. Tongues are wagging. You could get hurt, honey. I don't want that."

Andi straightened up and forced a smile. "Don't worry about *me*, big brother. I can take care of myself. Besides, if I don't go to school, everybody will say I was scared to show my face." *Which isn't too far from the truth*, she added silently.

Only one thing had lured Andi back to town. The music box. If she didn't return to school, she had no chance to work and pay off her mother's gift. She had already lost a precious week of wages, and her mother's birthday was drawing closer.

Andi jumped down from the buggy. Rosa followed right behind.

"If you need me," Justin said in parting, "I'll be in my office all day."

"I'll be fine," Andi assured him and headed for the schoolhouse.

"If *Señor* Justin knew the real reason you have come to town, he would take you back to the ranch *pronto*. Like this!" She snapped her fingers in Andi's face.

Andi pushed Rosa's hand away and set her jaw. Then she closed her eyes and sent up a silent prayer for courage. *Lord, You know I'd rather be back at the ranch right now. I'm doing this for my mother's gift. Please help me get through the next two weeks.*

Warm fingers slipped into her hand and squeezed it. "I'm praying, too," Rosa whispered.

Andi opened her eyes and flashed Rosa a grateful smile. She held tightly to her friend's hand. "Thanks."

Andi waited until the first bell rang before heading across the schoolyard. "No sense inviting questions right off," she told Rosa.

It took all her resolve to enter the schoolhouse and climb the empty steps to the upstairs classroom. When she and Rosa headed for their desks, the noisy pupils became still. All eyes turned toward Andi.

It was no trick to figure out that her classmates had been talking about her. She slid into her seat and sat in stony silence, staring at her desktop. The whispers began again, only not as loudly as before.

When silence fell a second time, Andi looked up. Johnny Wilson was slinking into his back-row seat. He obviously wanted to avoid his classmates too. His face looked haggard, and his eyes were rimmed in red. His usually slicked-back hair hung over his forehead in disarray. He shot Andi such a look of hatred that she caught her breath.

"It's not true, is it, Andi?" Cory Blake threw himself into his seat behind Andi.

The first question. Andi sighed and pulled her gaze away from Johnny. Cory was one of her best friends. She couldn't ignore him. "Is *what* not true?"

"The rumor going around town. The one that says you're making the whole thing up about seeing Peter. Some mean-spirited folks say you've got a grudge against the Wilson family."

Only against Johnny. "Why would anybody think that?" she said aloud. "I don't make up stories."

Cory shrugged. "I don't know. I'm just telling you what I heard."

"It's not true," Andi snapped. "Our families are friends."

Cory raised his hands and sat back in his seat. "No need to bite my head off. I believe you. But it's not gonna take long before this latest story makes its way around town. If I were you, I'd stay home."

Cory was right. Andi should have stayed home. But she was here now, and she wasn't going to run crying to Justin because a few busybodies were calling her a liar. She wracked her brain trying to think why anyone would believe she would lie about Peter. She'd never do that. She liked Peter. She liked the entire Wilson family, except for—

"This is probably Johnny's doing," she muttered. Although he appeared stupid and idle when it came to schoolwork, Johnny was deviously clever when thinking up ways to torment others.

The schoolmaster rang the tardy bell, and class began. The morning dragged. Andi couldn't keep focused on her schoolwork. Thankfully, Mr. Foster seemed to sense her distress and passed her by when it came time for her class to recite.

By the time the schoolmaster dismissed class for the noon recess, Andi was ready for a break. She snatched her dinner pail and clattered down the steps ahead of everyone. She wanted to find a spot where she wouldn't be pestered with questions. She didn't want to think about trials or lawyers or hostile classmates.

A few minutes later, Rosa plopped down beside her. "I will leave if you want to be alone."

"I don't mind if *you* stay." Andi bit into her peach.

"Are you really going to work at the mercantile today?" Rosa asked.

"You know it's the only reason I came to town," Andi replied. "I've got to work off the music box before the trial or I'll miss Mother's birthday."

Rosa frowned her disapproval. "You should not be here. You should be out at the ranch—away from Johnny, away from his ugly looks and mean talk. I do not believe any gift is worth what you are doing."

"My mother's gift is worth even putting up with Johnny Wilson."

"Did I hear my name?"

Andi glanced up to see Johnny towering over her. He was not smiling, nor had his expression changed from the way he'd looked at her before school. He stuck out his chin. "Congratulations, Andi. You tossed a hornets' nest into my family, and we're all getting stung. I hope you're satisfied."

Andi dropped her gaze to the ground. As much as she detested Johnny, she felt nothing but sympathy for the rest of his family. But she'd done nothing wrong. How could Johnny blame her for only telling what she saw?

"I know you haven't much use for me," Johnny continued, "but I never thought you would falsely accuse my brother just to get back at *me*."

Andi's head jerked up. "What are you talking about?"

"Shut up and listen. My father paces the floor at night, my mother cries, and Peter's treated like a common criminal. It's your fault."

"*My* fault? Peter's the one who did the killing. I only saw—"

Johnny dragged Andi to her feet. "Don't say that. Ever!" His eyes blazed. "Of course it's your fault. Is it a coincidence you 'saw' Peter with that drunk, Ben Decker, not more than two weeks after you said you'd pay me back?"

By now, a crowd of curious classmates had gathered in a loose ring around Andi and Johnny. They surged forward, eager to hear every word.

Andi's temper flared. "Pay you back? For what?"

Johnny narrowed his eyes. "Don't you remember our little encounter in the alley behind Goodwin's?"

Andi gaped at Johnny. Then she blushed as the pieces fell together. "How dare you! Do you think I'd hurt Peter because of *you*? Because you stole a lousy *kiss*?" She suddenly didn't care if the whole school knew about her humiliating encounter with Johnny. "I saw what I saw, and nobody can make me say anything different."

"You said you'd pay me back, and it looks like you have. But you won't get away with it. I told my father and the sheriff what you said to me that day in the alley. I also had a conversation with that big-city newspaper reporter. He was *real* interested in my story."

Andi swallowed. Hard. So, Mr. Harvey Wellin had found someone willing to talk to him. "Who cares? San Francisco's a long way from here. Besides, nobody will believe your dumb story, even if every newspaper in the state prints it."

But she knew that wasn't true. People would read it. They would believe it. People were always ready to believe the worst, especially if it created a sensation.

"My brother's not going to prison," Johnny growled. "No matter *who* you think you saw."

"The only thing that will keep Peter out of jail is if he's man enough to tell the truth!"

It was a mistake to challenge Johnny. He seized Andi's wrist and raised a fist. "So help me, Andi, if you weren't a girl, I'd give you—"

"Johnny!" Cory pushed his way through the small crowd. "Get away from her."

Jack Goodwin planted himself in front of Cory. "Stay out of this."

Cory shoved him aside. "Get out of my way, Jack."

For an answer, Jack threw himself at Cory, knocking him to the ground. Instantly, the school children abandoned Andi and Johnny and instead circled the two scuffling boys. "Fight! Fight!" they shouted.

Andi groaned. Could this day get any worse? Johnny was threatening to punch her, Jack and Cory were fighting, and the whole school was taking great delight in this unexpected diversion.

Johnny turned back to Andi, his fist still raised. "Now see what you've done. I've a mind to—"

Jack and Cory were still scuffling on the ground. They rolled into Johnny, knocking him forward. His fist plunged into Andi's stomach.

With an agonized cry, Andi doubled over and collapsed. She clutched her belly and tried to catch her breath. It came in huge gasps. Tears sprang to her eyes.

The fight between the two boys ended abruptly.

Cory fell to the ground beside her. "Are you all right?"

Andi ignored Cory. She looked up.

Johnny stood frozen. His face had drained of all color. "Andi, I . . . I didn't mean—"

"Get out of here, Johnny," Cory growled, standing to face the older boy.

Johnny shoved a meaty finger in Cory's chest. "It wasn't my fault." Then he turned tail and disappeared around the schoolhouse at a dead run.

Jack stood nearby, chewing on his lower lip and watching with dark, somber eyes. "It was an accident," he whispered. "Johnny didn't mean to hurt her."

Cory whirled on Jack. "If he hadn't been bothering Andi in the first place, none of this would have happened." He reached out his hand. "C'mon, Andi. I'll help you back to class."

Andi allowed Cory to help her stand, but she refused his offer to see her to the classroom. Instead, she staggered away from the schoolyard. She would not return to class. Not today.

Maybe not ever.

Chapter Twelve

UNEXPECTED HELP

A ndi pulled her knees to her chest and leaned back against the building on a side street behind Justin's office. She was certain no one could hear her, so she allowed herself the luxury of crying. Accident or not, Johnny had really hurt her.

A few minutes later, she rubbed her tear-streaked face against her sleeve and tried to stand. She clutched her stomach and took a few halting steps toward her brother's office. She wanted nothing more than to throw herself into Justin's strong, safe arms. He'd protect her from that rotten Johnny! He'd probably march right over to the Wilsons' and demand to see the rascal. Maybe Justin would punch him and . . .

Andi shook her head. No, Justin wouldn't punch him, but Chad would. She took two more steps, imagining with satisfaction Johnny's fate at the hands of her brothers.

Then reality hit her—hard. She paused and considered what would *really* happen if Justin saw her like this. *He'll take me home so fast it'll make my head spin. Mother won't let me step a foot off the ranch by myself until the trial. I won't be able to earn the music box.*

Andi set her jaw against the pain. She couldn't tell Justin what had happened, no matter how much she hurt. She'd have to pretend everything was fine. She took a deep breath and started walking away from her brother's office.

It was no use. She stumbled into a brick wall and slid to the ground. Tears of frustration sprang to her eyes. She buried her face across her knees and waited for the dull, throbbing pain to lessen.

"Hey, are you hurt?"

Andi raised her head. Young Robbie Decker stood above her. His britches were held up by one frayed suspender, and he was barefoot. Two bright, curious eyes shone in his dirty face. He was chewing on a piece of beef jerky. "You don't look so good," he said between bites. "What happened?"

The blunt question caught Andi off guard. "I got punched in the stomach."

"Ouch." Robbie winced. "I know what that feels like. It hurts somethin' fierce." He knelt beside her. "Who done it?"

"Johnny Wilson."

Robbie unleashed a torrent of back-alley words describing Johnny and finished with, "He ain't no gentleman. A gentleman *never* hits a girl, not even by accident."

Andi smiled weakly at the little boy's recital. "You better go. I'll be all right."

"I ain't gonna leave you here." Robbie stuffed the last of the jerky into his pocket and scooted closer to Andi. "You can lean on me. We'll go to my place. Meg can fix you a cup o' tea to settle your stomach." He put a thin arm around her waist and tugged. For a scrawny, underfed child, he was surprisingly strong.

What seemed like a long time later, Andi and her escort came upon a row of small, rundown shacks. None of them could have been larger than Andi's bedroom. Robbie led her through the door of his home. "Here we are."

Andi looked around. The place was small and dark, but seemed clean. The door and one window offered the only light. A pot-bellied stove stood next to the door, its stovepipe poking through an opening in the roof. A speckled, enamel coffee pot rested on the stove.

Andi found a seat on a battered fruit box. There was no table. No proper chairs. She glanced at the far wall. A girl lay sleeping on a collection of straw-filled burlap bags that served as a mattress.

"Megan!" Robbie shouted, shaking the girl awake. "We got company. Let's have some tea."

"Huh?" Megan sat up and rubbed her eyes. She scrambled to her feet when she saw Andi. Her mouth fell open.

Megan was a pretty girl, about Melinda's age, with soft brown eyes and a scattering of freckles across her thin face. Her hair was pulled back under a ragged scarf. She yanked a shawl around her shoulders and demanded, "What's *she* doin' here, Robbie?"

"I found her crying in an alley back of Tulare Street," the boy explained. "I brought her here for some of your tea. She's got a pain in her belly."

Megan shuffled to the stove and blew the tiny fire to life. Then she dipped water from a bucket into the enameled pot and faced Andi. "You shouldn't be here," she said in a tired voice. "The flappin' tongues in town have enough to jaw about without a visit here to add to their talk."

"You know who I am?"

Megan nodded. "You're the girl who saw our pa get killed and was fool enough to tell the sheriff about it." She sighed. "You shoulda kept your mouth shut."

Andi was stunned into silence.

"Not that I'm faultin' you. I know it musta been a shock to see something like that." Megan lowered her voice. "But when you saw who it was that killed Pa, you shoulda known there'd be trouble. Woulda been best if you'd let folks believe it was an accident." The girl let out a long, weary sigh. "It woulda been—sooner or later."

She looked so sad that Andi's heart ached as badly as her stomach.

Megan tightened the shawl around her shoulders and checked the water. "I feel sorry for you. The whole town's talkin' about it, you know."

Yes, Andi did know that. What she couldn't understand was Megan's attitude.

"Here's the tea things." Robbie held out a cracked china cup to his sister.

A few minutes later, Megan poured hot water into the cup. She added a few tea leaves and passed the steaming concoction to Andi. "Let it steep a bit."

"Thank you." Andi watched it darken up and then drank the tea slowly. She was surprised at how quickly her stomach began to feel better. When the cup was empty, Robbie offered her more.

Megan shook her head. "She better go. No good'll come of her bein' here."

Andi smiled at Robbie. "I feel much better now. You were right about the tea. Thanks for helping me."

Robbie beamed. "You rescued me from those two bullies the other day. 'Course I'd help you."

Megan walked Andi outside into the afternoon sunshine. "You're mighty bold to go up against the Wilsons, even though you're a fool for doin' it." She paused. "Can I ask you a question?"

Andi nodded.

"Why are you goin' against your own kind—one of your family's closest friends—on account of a worthless old drunk like Pa?"

Andi bit her lip and studied Megan's hurting expression. "Because it's the right thing to do. I have to tell what I saw."

"Even if the truth destroys a nice young man and his family?"

The question took Andi by surprise. "I . . . I don't know what you mean."

"Look here, Miss Carter," Megan said. "I think real high of you for stickin' to your principles and all, but Pa ain't worth the trouble. He's dead, and me and Robbie won't miss him much."

"That's for sure," Robbie muttered.

Megan shushed him. "I hate to see your family and the Wilsons get torn up on account of Pa. I heard your own brother's not too happy about what you're doing."

Andi winced. News certainly traveled fast in this town. But it was true. Mitch hadn't said more than two words to her all last week.

Megan took a deep breath. "I want you to know that it's all right with me if you decide you didn't see who killed Pa, after all." She ducked her head and slipped back into the shack.

Robbie said good-bye and followed his sister through the open door.

Andi stood still. *Why would she say that?* It was as if Megan *wanted* Andi to change her story. She frowned in confusion, took a step, and nearly collided with the newspaper reporter, Harvey Wellin.

He reached out a hand to steady her. "Pardon me, Miss Carter."

Andi pulled away. "What are you doing here?"

"Trying to get my story."

"You're following me!"

He bowed and grinned. "Guilty as charged."

Andi flushed, outraged. What had he heard with his spying? She turned her back on the annoying young man and headed for the main part of town.

He ran to catch up. "Pretty soon I won't need an interview."

Andi stopped and faced the reporter. She watched uneasily as he pulled out his notepad, licked his pencil point, and began to scribble. She frowned. "What are you writing?"

"Let's see. Playing hooky from school to hobnob with the victim's family. Is it possible you know more about this than you're telling?" He looked up.

"Go away. Go back to San Francisco."

Mr. Wellin chuckled. "Give me a few minutes of your time, darlin', and I'll do just that. What do you say?"

Instead of answering, Andi took off running down the street, only dimly aware of the ache in her belly. Mr. Harvey Wellin would see to it that everybody in Fresno knew where she'd been this afternoon.

When Justin found out, he'd skin her alive.

Chapter Thirteen

ANDI STIRS UP A SENSATION

A ndi entered the mercantile with a sagging spirit. She hoped
Mr. Goodwin would find something for her to do the rest of
the afternoon. Keeping busy was the only way she could calm her
churning thoughts.

Before she looked for the shopkeeper, she slipped to the display
window and leaned close to the small music box. "If you only knew
what I've gone through today," she whispered, running her fingers
along the polished wood. "You'd better be worth it. I don't know
how long I can—"

"I declare, Emily!" A loud voice broke into Andi's musing. "Have
you see this week's edition of the *Expositor*?" There was the sound of
swishing skirts as a woman strolled past, one aisle over.

Andi ducked behind the shelves of dry goods and headed for the
back of the store. She had no desire to listen to Mrs. King and Mrs.
Evans gossip.

Mrs. King's next words froze Andi mid step. "Indeed I have, Millie
Evans. It's a crying shame, that's what it is. That poor young man
accused of killing a drunk, while his heartbroken mother grieves
day and night. I called on Alice Wilson this morning, and goodness!
She's aged ten years this past week."

"You don't say!"

"I *do* say," Mrs. King huffed. "Peter Wilson is such a nice boy. I don't understand why Sheriff Tate had to arrest him in the first place—all on account of a silly prank. It's criminal, that's what it is."

Mrs. Evans sniffed her agreement.

In her mind's eye, Andi could see the old biddy rising to her full height of just over five feet, lifting her chin, and delivering her next statement with the air of Queen Victoria.

"What I don't understand, Emily, is why Elizabeth Carter does nothing to curb her girl's loose tongue."

The blood drained from Andi's face at the mention of her mother's name. Her head spun. *Don't faint!* She clapped a hand over her mouth to keep from crying out.

"Perhaps Elizabeth doesn't realize the harm," Mrs. King replied. "If Andrea were my child, I'd turn her over my knee and warm her backside good and proper. Then I'd march her down to Sheriff Tate's office and put an end to this foolishness."

"Perhaps we should call on Elizabeth this afternoon and suggest just that."

"An excellent idea, Millie. I believe I . . ."

Andi fled without hearing the rest of Mrs. King's sentence. She slipped into the back storeroom and found an empty corner. *This is the worst day of my life.* Too angry to cry, her whole body shook with rage and shame. She leaned her head back against the wall and stared at the rough planks in the ceiling.

Mr. Goodwin found her there fifteen minutes later. "Andi! What in the world are you doing in my storeroom, lurking in a corner?"

Andi jumped to her feet. "I'm hiding from Mrs. Evans and Mrs. King. They were saying all kinds of horrible things about—"

"Yes, I caught a portion of it while they were making their purchases." Mr. Goodwin grimaced through his mustache. "I want you to know I gave them a piece of my mind. They left in a hurry after that. It's safe to come out." He crooked a finger at her. "Why don't you give me a hand this afternoon? That ought to keep your mind off the town's busybodies. The store is in disarray from the weekend, and I'm still not caught up from my buying trip."

Andi followed Mr. Goodwin out of the stockroom. "I'm sorry I couldn't be here last Saturday to help you with the unpacking."

"I understand completely, Andi. An inquest is no fun." He motioned her toward the counters. "I won't ask what you're doing out of school this afternoon, but perhaps it would be best if you stayed home until this all blows over."

"You know I can't do that. By the time it's over, my mother's birthday will be past. I want to earn the music box before then."

Mr. Goodwin nodded his understanding. "All right. If you're willing to brave the town's gossips, I'd say you're pretty set on working." He handed her a dusting cloth and headed back to the storeroom. "Holler if you need anything."

Andi took the rag and went to work. She was grateful for the chance to keep her mind on a task, and she headed right for the messy counters. It didn't take long to put them in order. Working her way along the shelves, she came at last to the main counter, where the cash register rested.

The *Fresno Weekly Expositor* lay spread out next to the register. She began to gather up the pages. "Mr. Goodwin," she called toward the storeroom, "what do you want me to do with the—"

Andi broke off when her gaze fell on the page she held in her hand. Staring back at her was a headline that made her stomach turn over.

"Oh no, it can't be . . ." Her voice trailed off as she scanned the front page for the full story. When she read the byline—"by Harvey Wellin, *San Francisco Chronicle*"—she wanted to scream.

Andi was a fast reader. By the time she worked her way through the lengthy article, her heart was pounding. No wonder Mrs. Evans and Mrs. King had spoken so harshly.

The *Expositor* had printed Johnny's story—every lousy detail— just like he'd boasted. He'd told the entire town about his argument with Andi three weeks ago, and how she'd promised to pay him back for his brash kiss. According to Johnny, she had clearly found a way to take her revenge.

"This is terrible," Andi murmured.

Johnny had left nothing out of their encounter, not even his and Jack's bullying of little Robbie Decker. Every word was true. It made the rest of Johnny's story sound reasonable.

Andi dropped the paper to the counter. She expected a big-city newspaper to report grisly details and half-truths, but never in her wildest imagination did she think the *Expositor*, her own town's paper, would go so far as to print hearsay and rumors.

But the cold, hard facts, as she painfully discovered, were not what readers wanted to hear. Most of the article focused on Ben Decker's sinful lifestyle and how the town now had one less drunk. The paper reminded its readers of Peter Wilson's upstanding character and sympathized with his present misfortune as the target of someone's revenge.

"This is so unfair!" Andi sputtered. "Maybe I should talk to Mr. Harvey Wellin, after all. I could think of a thing or two to even things up."

"I'm sorry you had to see this." Mr. Goodwin's voice jerked Andi from her daze. "That good-for-nothing son of Wilson's has really done it this time. I'm ashamed to say my Jack had anything to do with it. You probably noticed his name right there beside Johnny's."

Andi nodded. The *Expositor* had been painfully clear. Jack had backed up Johnny's story all the way. "I don't care what anybody in San Francisco thinks, but *this*?" She wadded the front section up in a ball and slammed it down on the counter. "Now the whole town knows about . . . knows about . . ." Her throat tightened. She couldn't go on.

Andi suddenly wanted to finish cleaning and go home. She gathered the rest of the newspaper and began folding it. "Where do you want me to put it?" she asked.

Before Mr. Goodwin could answer, she noticed the word *Carter* on the back page. "What now?" she muttered.

It was an editorial. A boring one, too, until she read, "It is our hope that the Carters will come to their senses and take the situation in hand in order to avoid a needless smearing of our esteemed banker, Charles Wilson, and his family. That a childish prank could lead to so serious a charge as the taking of human life is a crime in itself, especially when one remembers the victim was—"

The paper disappeared from her hands. Mr. Goodwin tucked it under his arm. "You don't need to read any more of that."

"Did you see what he wrote?"

"Don't take it to heart, Andi. George Fleming's editorials are meant to stir up a sensation. That's what sells newspapers. It'll die down."

"Not soon enough. After today, I won't be able to show my face in town."

"Nonsense." Mr. Goodwin took Andi by the shoulders and steered her toward the door. "It's getting late. Go on home and forget about this. I don't want to hear any silly talk about not coming into town on account of a trashy newspaper article. You work for me now. I expect you here tomorrow, same time as usual."

"I thought you told me I should stay home."

Mr. Goodwin grinned. "I've changed my mind, girl. Believe me, no one who shops here will dare open his mouth in my hearing. Now, you'd better get going, before Justin wonders where you are."

Andi gave in. "All right. I'll see you tomorrow." Downcast, she made her way back to Justin's office to catch a ride home.

"Andi, I'd like to ask you a couple of questions." Justin slapped the reins, and the horse broke into a fast trot.

Andi waited. It didn't take much figuring to guess what kind of questions her brother had in mind. So far the ride home had been uncomfortably quiet. When she'd learned that Justin had sent Rosa home with one of the ranch hands, Andi knew she was in for a big-brother talk. She was not looking forward to it.

"First of all," Justin said, "tell me you weren't at the Decker place this afternoon."

Andi squirmed under Justin's pleading gaze. If she told him she was there, he'd want to know why. When he learned the reason, she'd find herself back at the ranch for good. If she didn't tell him, he'd jump to his own conclusions about her visit.

"So it's true," Justin said when she didn't answer. "You *were* there. I really hoped it was nothing more than idle gossip." He gave her a disappointed look. "Let's see if I've got this straight. You play hooky from school and find yourself in the home of the recent murder victim. You enjoy a cup of tea and some light conversation with the children of the deceased. Furthermore, when confronted by a newspaper reporter, you run away, making it appear as if you have something to hide."

"How did you find out?"

"I had a visit from Harvey Wellin, our nosy and very determined newspaper reporter. He was hoping to pry a story out of me in exchange for keeping your little afternoon adventure a secret."

Andi's shoulders slumped. "What did you tell him?"

"Absolutely nothing. I sent him on his way." Then he continued. "Another thing. What's all this between you and Johnny Wilson?"

"Nothing."

"That's no answer. Did you confront him in the alley behind Goodwin's a few weeks ago?"

Andi nodded.

"Is it true he kissed you?" Justin clearly didn't care if his question embarrassed her.

Andi's face burned with shame.

Justin let out a long, slow breath, as if he couldn't believe he was having this conversation. "I can see by your face that he did. So I have one more question. Did you threaten to pay Johnny back because he kissed you?"

Andi wanted to crawl in a hole. "Justin—"

"Did you?"

She nodded, cringing at the memory of her hasty words. "I didn't mean it, Justin. Honest, I didn't. I was just so angry. Johnny's a beast. I punched him in the nose and hollered at him and—" She broke off when Justin pulled the buggy to a stop in the middle of the road. "What's the matter?"

Justin let go of the reins and gave Andi his full attention. "So the article on the front page of the *Expositor* has Johnny quoting you correctly?"

Andi clasped her hands in her lap and said nothing.

"Answer me."

As much as she wanted to scream a denial, she couldn't. "Yes," she whispered.

"Why didn't you tell me?"

Andi shrugged. "I stood up to him, he kissed me, I gave him a bloody nose, and it was over. I didn't want anybody to know. Johnny Wilson is disgusting."

"Well, it's not over any longer," Justin said. "Your silly threat—whether you meant it or not—has put this whole incident in a new light."

Andi wrinkled her forehead. What did it matter if she'd yelled at Johnny, or promised to pay him back, or anything else that gossipy newspaper article had said? The truth was the truth.

Or was it? "What do you mean?" she asked.

"Are you *sure* you saw Peter fighting with Ben Decker? It didn't happen any other way? You didn't stumble across the dead man, see Peter a few minutes later, and jump to a conclusion? What Johnny did to you has no bearing on what you saw?"

"Of course not!" Andi exclaimed, shocked.

"Are you *certain* you didn't see someone else? A stranger you couldn't identify? Someone who looked like Peter? Those back alleys are full of shadows that time of day."

"Why do you keep asking me? Don't you believe me anymore?" She picked up the reins. "I want to go home."

Justin snatched the reins from her hands and set them aside. Then he reached out and pulled his sister around to face him.

Andi caught her breath at the look on his face. He looked discouraged, upset, and worried—all mixed together in an expression that frightened her.

"The reason I keep asking, young lady, is because very soon someone else will be asking you these same questions," Justin said. "But he won't be asking them as nicely as I am. You'll be on the witness stand with most of the town looking on. Peter Wilson's attorney will try his best to make you look like a foolish, empty-headed little girl—a girl who made up a story out of spite. And between your actions this afternoon and your words to Johnny, I almost agree with him."

Andi twisted away from her brother's grip. "Why are you talking so mean?"

Justin picked up the reins and slapped the horse. The buggy lurched, and Andi fell back against the seat. "It's because I don't like surprises. No lawyer does. Your trouble with Johnny has fallen neatly into the Wilsons' laps. Peter's lawyer is no fool. He'll tear your testimony apart and twist it around until he has you so confused you won't know *what* to say. I've seen him do it. It's not a pretty sight. Now, if there's anything else you've *forgotten* to tell me or the district attorney, you'd better remember in a hurry."

His dark blue gaze bored into her. "Is there?"

Andi's eyes filled with angry tears. She hadn't meant to keep anything back. She never dreamed Johnny would dig up that horrid experience and use it to damage her testimony in court.

Everything was so mixed up!

"Oh, Justin, you told me I just had to get up, say my piece, and sit down. You said I had nothing to worry about."

"That was before I read the newspaper. Now answer my question."

Andi turned stubborn. She folded her arms across her chest. "I told you what I saw, and it has nothing to do with what happened with Johnny. If you want to believe that bully instead of your own sister, I reckon I can't stop you."

Justin's voice softened. "That's not it at all." He guided the horse and buggy up the road to the ranch house. "I'm worried—more than you know. Maybe I pushed you harder than I should have, but you have an unpleasant ordeal ahead. I want you to be prepared for it."

Ten minutes later, Justin pulled into the yard. He reached out to give Andi a hug, but she pushed him away and jumped out of the buggy before it rolled to a stop.

Chapter Fourteen

A HOUSE DIVIDED

Supper was horrible. Andi didn't eat much and said less, still upset over her encounter with Johnny and the article in the newspaper. Justin's no-nonsense talk hadn't helped her mood either. She pushed her food around on her plate and worried about how she'd make it through the rest of the school week.

An idea popped into her head. Perhaps Mr. Goodwin would let her work full days. *I could avoid school and earn the music box in—*

"Biscuits and jam are your favorite, Andrea. Why are you picking at them?"

Andi dropped her fork onto the mess she'd made of her supper. "I'm sorry, Mother. I'm just not very hungry."

She looked around at her family. The usual cheerful banter about the events of the day—a funny incident with the cowhands, a new project Melinda had begun, or Chad teasing Andi because she'd grumbled about school—was missing. It was as silent and uncomfortable as a group of strangers sharing a meal.

Just then, Mitch strode into the dining room whistling a tune. He pulled out his chair and sat down with a smile. "Sorry I'm late. I got tied up in town." He spread his napkin in his lap, bowed his head for a quick blessing, and began to dish up his plate.

"It's nice to see someone in good spirits this evening," Mother remarked.

"How about sharing with the rest of us?" Chad passed Mitch the potatoes. "It's as cheerful around here as the middle of an anthrax epidemic."

"I spent a couple of hours talking with Peter this afternoon," Mitch said. He helped himself to a heaping serving of mashed potatoes and reached for the gravy.

Justin lowered his fork. "And . . . ?"

"Well, Justin, you know how badly I feel about what's happening. I want to help Peter the best I can by keeping up his spirits, listening to him, just being there." He paused. "It seemed like the right thing to do. A fellow can't abandon his friends, you know."

"That's mighty loyal of you, little brother," Chad said. He exchanged a wary glance with Justin.

Mitch popped a large piece of roast beef into his mouth and chewed contentedly for a few minutes. Then he grinned. "After talking to Peter, I think I have good news. We spent some time trying to piece together the missing hour from that Friday afternoon. You know, when we split up to get ready for our trip. Peter hopes that between the two of us, we'll be able to remember enough to give him a chance."

"A chance?" Melinda piped up with a puzzled frown. "A chance for what?"

"Why, a chance to clear his name. Isn't that what we all want?" Mitch stabbed at his beef and looked at Andi. "Isn't that what *you* want, Sis?"

"Yes," Andi whispered.

"I was under the impression that what we'd like is the truth," Justin said. "Have you any idea what it will mean if you manage to fill in that missing hour for Peter?"

Mitch helped himself to a biscuit. "I assume it'll mean Peter might avoid serving time in prison."

Chad pointed his fork at Mitch. "No, it means you'll be calling our sister a liar. Or didn't that occur to you?"

"I don't think she's lying," Mitch said. "I think she's just honestly mistaken."

Chad's fist came down on the table with a crash that rattled the dishes. "Oh, that's brilliant, Mitch! Did you think of that before or *after* you read the article in the *Expositor*?"

Mitch jumped up. "Now hold on, Chad. I haven't read the paper. Browning asked if I knew anything that might help—"

"Browning?" Justin demanded. "*Maxwell* Browning?" His voice betrayed his dismay at this news. "You've spoken with Peter's attorney?"

Mitch nodded and returned to his seat. "He stopped by the Wilsons' when I was there this afternoon. So?"

"You know he'll put you on the stand, don't you? You'll be up there just long enough to tear Andi's testimony apart." Justin frowned. "That should make good copy for the *Expositor*. I can see the headline now: 'Carter Family Divided over Upcoming Murder Trial.'"

Mitch stood up and threw his napkin on the table. "Is that all you care about, Justin? Bad publicity for this family? Don't you understand? Peter might go to *prison*."

"That will be enough," Mother broke in. She looked at her youngest son. "I understand your loyalty to Peter. He's a good friend. We all love him. However"—her voice turned firm—"this family stands together. I don't care what the papers say. They've said more than enough already."

"That's for sure," Chad muttered under his breath.

Mother ignored him. "I only want the truth. Andrea says she saw Peter kill Ben Decker. That ought to be good enough for us, and for *you*, Mitchell. Peter Wilson's attorney will use your divided loyalties to remember events the way he wants you to. He's not interested in the truth, only in clearing his client's name." She took a deep breath. "It's important that you stay away from the Wilsons and their lawyer."

Without a word, Mitch stalked out of the dining room.

Andi leaped from her chair. "Mitch!"

"Let him be, Andrea," Mother warned.

Andi swallowed and watched her brother slam through the dining room door. Then she sat down and stared at her plate of now-cold food. *All I did was tell the truth, and now everything's in a muddle. We can't even have a pleasant supper anymore. Oh, what am I going to do?*

Andi ran the comb through the last tangle of Taffy's mane and stepped back. Never had her horse looked so beautiful. Andi had brushed her until her coat shone as bright as a newly minted gold piece. Every snarl had been combed out of Taffy's cream-colored mane and tail.

Andi gave a low, admiring whistle and dropped the mane comb into the grooming box. Then she crossed over to the other side of the stall and fell to the straw, worn out.

Immediately, a small black puppy jumped into her lap and began licking her face. His wagging tail made swishing noises in the hay. Andi gathered the dog in her arms and buried her face in his soft fur. "What do you think, Scout? Isn't Taffy beautiful?"

The puppy's answer was a *slap, slap, slap* of his tail against her legs and a wet kiss.

She giggled. "I guess that means yes."

"Andi?"

She looked up. Mitch stood hanging over the half-door of Taffy's stall. A crooked smile covered his face.

"Listen, Sis," he began sheepishly, "I'm sorry I got so riled at supper." He straightened up and reached for the latch. "May I join you?"

Andi shrugged. "I reckon."

Mitch let himself into the stall and crossed over to where Andi sat in the straw. He kneeled down and scratched the dog behind the ears. "Nice pup. Does he have a name?"

"I named him Scout for now, but Mother hasn't said I can keep him." She sighed. "Actually, I don't know if I even *want* to keep him. Every time I see him, I remember what happened that Friday." She hugged the puppy tighter. "It's not this little fellow's fault, but I don't know if I want to be reminded."

"Good point." Mitch scratched the puppy once more and settled himself in the hay next to Andi. Then he picked up a piece of straw, twirled it between his fingers, and spoke. "Andi, I want to—"

"Mitch," Andi interrupted, "I've been thinking. If you want me to, I'll go to the sheriff first thing tomorrow morning and tell him I made a mistake. It really *was* awfully gloomy in that alley. If you're so sure it can't be Peter, well then"—she paused and took a deep breath—"maybe you're right. Maybe I was mistaken. Anyway, I'll do it for you. I can't stand seeing our family torn apart over this. I want it to end, so we can all be happy again."

Mitch sat quietly, until Andi could stand his silence no longer. "Mitch, shall I—"

"No," came his soft reply. "I read the paper tonight. It says some mighty wild things about you, things that make me want to punch somebody in the nose. Folks might say you've made a mistake, but *nobody* better say you made up something purely for spite." He closed his eyes and leaned against the wall. "This whole thing is tearing me apart. But as much as I hate to admit it, Mother's right. If you say you saw Peter, then that's good enough for me."

Andi studied her brother's handsome but troubled face. Mitch was her good-natured, easygoing brother. She could always count on him to take her side during her frequent arguments with Chad, even when she was in the wrong. Because of his loyalty and his willingness to find the good in folks, he had plenty of friends. Andi could easily see how Mitch must be agonizing over Peter's plight.

When he opened his eyes, she said, "I saw him, Mitch. But the more folks tell me I'm mistaken, the more I'm starting to wonder. Then when *you* start saying I'm wrong . . ."

She began to cry. "It's been such a Jonah day! First, I had to put up with Johnny Wilson's bullying at school. Then the newspaper reporter, Harvey Wellin, chased me down and tried to make me talk to him. Later on I heard two old biddies criticizing Mother on account of me. On the way home from school, Justin gave me one of those big-brother talks he's so good at. Worst of all, the *Expositor* printed Johnny's story for the whole town to read!"

Mitch put an arm around Andi's shoulder and hugged her. "Forgive me, Sis, for not believing you. I was so busy worrying about Peter that I didn't realize how hard all of this must be for you." He sighed. "I appreciate that you're willing to go to the sheriff and change your story for me, but I can't let you do it. Stick to the truth and tell what you saw. It's the only way."

"What if you get called to the witness stand?"

"I promise I won't say anything that hurts your testimony." He let Andi go, stood up, and brushed the straw from his trousers. "The Bible says the truth will set us free, and I believe it will. The truth's going to set *all* of us free. Peter too." He grinned. "Only Peter doesn't know it yet. Come on." He reached out a hand to help Andi from the straw. "Let's go inside. It's getting chilly."

Andi grasped her brother's hand and rose to her feet. Suddenly, in a burst of gratitude, she threw her arms around Mitch and gave him a hug. "Thanks, Mitch," she whispered. "I love you."

Chapter Fifteen

A CHANGE OF HEART

The next couple of weeks crawled by for Andi. She had held out a faint hope that once Johnny stirred up the town with his story, the sensation would die down and folks would wait for the trial before they started gossiping again. But it was not so. Tongues wagged even faster than before, lines were drawn, and the town stayed divided.

Things took a slight turn for the better at school, however. Johnny stopped coming to class the middle of the second week. The pupils breathed a collective sigh of relief, and Andi's spirits rose a notch. Even if a few of her classmates didn't believe her testimony, Andi was still well-liked—much more so than Johnny the bully.

With Johnny out of the way, the schoolroom settled down to almost normal. At least Mr. Foster held his pupils on a tight rein, which kept whispers to a minimum.

After her disastrous encounter with Johnny in the schoolyard, Andi figured it was better to stay indoors during recess. She watched the noon ball games from the second-story window, with loyal Rosa by her side. Time dragged so slowly that Andi could hardly stand it.

As soon as school dismissed each afternoon, Andi bid Rosa a quick good-bye and hurried to the safety of Goodwin's Mercantile. The shopkeeper always greeted her with a smile and a lemon drop.

On this particular Friday, Andi's drooping spirits perked up. She had done the arithmetic, and today the music box would be hers. Ten dollars and ninety-five cents—paid in full. For the first time in weeks, her thoughts drifted away from the upcoming trial and focused on the gift she had worked so hard to buy. She paused at the mercantile window and admired the music box before going inside.

"Another hour and you'll be mine," Andi told it through the glass. "Just in time, too. The trial's next Tuesday. You have no idea what I've gone through in order to buy you. I'm going to take you home, wrap you up real nice, and hide you under my bed. Then on Monday I'm going to stay home from school and just rest." Relief swept through her. "Best of all, I won't have to put up with Jack any longer."

"Who are you talking to?"

Andi scowled and faced Jack. "Quit sneaking up on me."

Jack peered past Andi into the shop's window. "You're always looking at the same old boring stuff. Nothing new. Nothing interesting. Now you're talking to it. Why? What's so interesting? That dumb kerosene lamp?" He grinned.

"As if I'd tell *you*," Andi retorted. She narrowed her eyes. "Don't you have work to do?"

"I reckon I could ask you the same question, seeing how Pa was so foolish as to hire you in the first place." He tapped the window pane. "Why are you so all-fired interested in that stuff in the window?"

"None of your business," Andi snapped.

Jack shook his head. "I can't figure you out, Andi. If it was me the whole town was talking about, I'd stay as far away from here as I could. I wouldn't like nobody calling *me* a liar. How do you stand it? Unless, of course"—his voice grew soft—"you really *are* one."

Andi pressed her lips together. Whenever Mr. Goodwin stepped into the back room, Jack pestered her. He made sure they worked together every day so he could prod her into changing her story. Andi suspected Johnny was behind Jack's questions. Jack was brash and unthinking, but he'd never been cruel.

And he'd never called Andi names before. That hurt.

"I don't take to anyone calling Mitch Carter's sister a liar," a new voice broke in. "I suggest you apologize, and be quick about it."

Andi and Jack forgot their quarrel and turned around as one. Peter Wilson stood a few yards away, holding what looked like a shopping list. He frowned at Jack and waited.

"I-I'm sorry, Andi." Jack stumbled over his apology. He gaped at Peter, eyes wide. "Why aren't you in . . . I mean . . . aren't you sup-posed to be . . . ?"

"In jail?" Peter finished for him. "I've been home since the hear-ing, staying pretty much to myself. My father bailed me out." He shrugged. "The trial's next Tuesday, and I'm not going anywhere. Besides, Sheriff Tate's meals leave a lot to be desired." He looked at Andi. "I didn't expect to see you here. How are you doing?"

Andi hadn't expected to run into Peter either. She remembered how upset Justin had been when he found out she'd visited Megan Decker. What would he say if he saw her *now*? "Should you even be talking to me?"

"Probably not." Peter let out a long, regretful sigh. "I've read the papers, Andi. I'm sorry."

"*You're* sorry?" Jack frowned. "What have you got to be sorry for?"

Peter ignored him. "Listen, Andi. I feel like a real skunk the way things have turned out. I've had plenty of time to think it over these past few weeks—first sitting alone in jail and now when I see the whole town in an uproar. I can't eat. I can't sleep." He slumped. "But it's too late to do anything about it now."

Andi saw guilt and misery etched on Peter's face. If only he'd tell the truth! "It's *not* too late. Talk to Justin. Please."

Peter held up a hand to stop her words. "Things have gotten out of hand, I'm afraid. My father . . . well, he's bound and determined to see me cleared of all charges." He looked ashamed. "I tried to tell him everything the other day, but he wouldn't listen. Instead, he became even more determined to clear me."

"The sheriff will listen," Andi said. "Tell him. Tell him right now."

Peter shook his head. "Don't you see? Father and Mr. Browning, that big-city lawyer, won't let me. They think I want to change my plea only to protect you from having to testify, because I don't want to see you hurt. Father won't listen to the truth now, even from me. And he won't let me 'throw away my life,' as he puts it, on account of one mistaken little girl."

"But—"

"Father and Mr. Browning have told the sheriff as much," he interrupted, "so it's no use going to him at this point. There are so many stories circulating around town that only the court can straighten it out. I just wanted to warn you, Andi. Father is confident I'll be found 'not guilty.' So go ahead and tell what you saw. My father"—he cleared his throat—"is not himself. I'm afraid for him." He touched the brim of his hat in farewell and entered the mercantile.

Jack let out a long, low whistle. "Well, what do you make of that?"

Andi stared at Peter's back as he disappeared into the store. "I think he was apologizing for not telling the truth."

Jack followed Andi's gaze. "Are you telling me that Peter, after all this time, suddenly decides he really *did* kill Ben Decker?"

Andi wanted to shake the boy. "Yes, that's exactly what I'm telling you, Jack. You heard him yourself just now. I've been saying it all along, but the only person you ever listen to is Johnny. Whatever that bully tells you to think or do or say, you jump right to it. Don't you ever think for yourself?"

"But Peter c-couldn't have done it," Jack stammered. "I mean, Johnny's so sure and . . . and it's me backing up his story about you paying him back, and . . . well, Peter's a swell fellow and . . . ." Jack bit his lip. "I'm in way over my head, Andi. I've *got* to back Johnny up. I don't have a choice."

Andi clenched her fists. "You *always* have a choice, Jack. Just like Peter does. He could go to the sheriff and tell him the truth. Maybe it wouldn't fix things up and we'd still have to go to court, but he could do it. But he's a coward. And so are you. I can't believe we used to be friends!" She gave Jack a shove that nearly sent him through the window of his father's store. Then she stomped into the mercantile to begin work.

Andi snagged an apron from the hook, tied it around her waist, and grabbed the broom. Her hands shook. She slammed through the screen door and began sweeping the walk. Dust flew as Andi slid the broom back and forth along the wooden planks. It felt good to whack at the dirt. She wished she could whack some sense into Johnny with it. Or better still, Jack.

She paused and looked around. Jack had disappeared.

"He's always taking off and leaving me with all the work." She dragged the broom to the edge of the wooden sidewalk and peered into the alley. Jack was deep in conversation with Johnny near a stack of crates a stone's throw away. Johnny flailed his arms in the air. Jack shook his head and started to leave, but Johnny wrenched him back.

Andi leaned the broom against the front of the mercantile and crept around the corner to hear better. She caught only snatches of the boys' exchange.

"Wait." Johnny drew a small, shiny object from his pocket, but Andi couldn't make out what it was. "It's yours if you want it."

Jack pocketed the item and motioned to Johnny. The two scuttled farther into the alley, out of Andi's sight.

"I wonder what they're up to now," Andi muttered. "Nothing good, I'm sure." She stepped onto the walkway, picked up the broom, and went back to work.

Andi waited impatiently for a customer to pay Mr. Goodwin for his goods. Her last day of work was over. The music box would soon be in her hands. She stood behind the counter next to the shopkeeper and wrapped the farmer's purchases in brown paper and tied them up with a piece of twine.

"Here you go, sir," she said with a smile. "Have a good evening."

The farmer didn't look at Andi. He grunted a short "evenin'" to Mr. Goodwin, gathered up his packages, and ambled toward the door.

Andi felt like she'd been slapped. Come what may during the trial, nothing could be worse than the unfriendly stares that followed her around town.

Mr. Goodwin looked at her kindly. "It won't be long, Andi. A few more days." Then he grinned. "Are you waiting for something?"

The store's clock read five o'clock on the dot. Andi would have to hurry to keep Justin from looking for her. "It's Friday, Mr. Goodwin. Pay day." She smiled back. "My last pay day, right?"

Mr. Goodwin chuckled. "Yes. Now run along and get what you earned."

Andi dashed to the window and gathered up her precious music box. Hugging the gift, she returned to Mr. Goodwin and beamed at him. "Thanks for letting me work off the price of the music box. You probably would have been better off with somebody who could work longer hours. So I really appreciate you hiring me."

Mr. Goodwin's eyebrows shot up. "You earned your music box fair and square. Not only that, but during the past few weeks Jack has started pulling his weight around here more, so I've been fine. If you ever need another job, come and see me first. You're a good worker, and your mother is a lucky woman. I wish I could see her face when she opens this gift."

He nodded at her attire. "You can leave that apron in the back. Just toss it in the bin when you go by."

Andi waved a cheerful good-bye to the shopkeeper and entered the back room. She set the music box down while she untied her apron for the last time and threw it in the bin.

Then she saw Jack. He was sitting on top of a large barrel, drinking a glass of iced lemonade. Whatever he'd been plotting with Johnny had not kept him away too long.

"Good-bye, Jack," she said. "You'll be happy to hear it's good-bye for good."

Jack set his glass down. "What do you mean?"

"I finished working for your father." She pointed to the music box resting on a small barrel near the bin. "My mother's birthday is next week. I've been working off that music box as a gift. Now it's mine."

"Why not just ask somebody for the money? Your family's rich enough. Your brothers would probably give you anything you asked for."

Andi wanted to laugh. Jack knew nothing about how things worked on the Circle C. "That's not true." She shook her head. "You don't understand."

"I reckon not." He held out his glass. "Want some lemonade?"

"No, I really need to go. It's getting late."

"Aw, come on. I made it myself. Have a drink."

Andi frowned. "Why are you being so nice all of a sudden? You were a beast just an hour ago. Then you disappeared." She gestured toward the back door. "What were you and Johnny hatching out in the alley?"

Jack's face paled. "Were you spying on us?"

Andi shrugged and took the glass. "For a minute. I saw Johnny hand you something and then you both slunk off."

Jack let out a long breath that to Andi looked like relief . . . and something else. Was it guilt? Uncertainty?

Andi let it go and sipped the lemonade. It was best not to try too hard to figure Jack out these days. Thank goodness she was finished having to put up with him.

The drink was surprisingly refreshing. "It's good, Jack. Not too sweet. Not too sour. Thanks."

"You know what?" Jack gave her an odd look. "That's the first nice thing you've said to me in ages."

"Offering me lemonade is the first nice thing *you've* done since you started going around with Johnny. It almost feels like old times." She smiled at him. A real smile.

Jack groaned and turned away. It was clear something was bothering him.

"What's wrong?" Andi asked. "You look ill."

Jack sucked in a sharp breath and slid off the barrel. He snatched the glass of lemonade from Andi. "You better go. Now. Take your music box and leave." He shoved her toward the front of the store. *"Hurry."*

Andi planted her feet. She wasn't going anywhere. "What in the world is wrong with you? Why do I have to—"

"Just *leave*," Jack whispered. He looked frightened.

The door to the back alley flew open. Johnny Wilson stood on the steps, his hands clasped behind his back. "Not so fast, buddy. Do you think I'd hand over that pearl-handled pistol without making sure you were following through on your end of the bargain?"

He yanked his hand around and held up a fistful of long, coarse, cream-colored hair. "Andi, if you want to see Taffy, you better come with us. And you better come quick and quiet-like."

Chapter Sixteen

A FRIGHTENING CHOICE

A ndi stumbled backward and caught herself against a barrel. The shock of seeing part of Taffy's mane in Johnny's filthy hand knocked the breath from her lungs. "You don't have Taffy. It's a trick."

Andi's head spun. Nobody could ride out to the Circle C and help themselves to a stabled horse. Especially during broad daylight. Johnny *must* be lying.

"You think so?" Johnny crowded into the store's back room and dangled the hank of mane in her face. "Go ahead then. Yell for Jack's pa. Or walk through that door. I won't stop you."

Andi didn't move. She couldn't take the chance. What if he was telling the truth?

Johnny grasped her wrist. "Let's go." He hauled her out of the building, down the steps, and deeper into the alley behind the mercantile.

Johnny led Andi to a pile of old lumber and discarded wagon wheels, where two horses were tied. A minute later, Jack appeared and untied his horse.

"Where have you been?" Johnny demanded.

"Making it look like Andi went home," Jack snapped. "Where did you think I was?"

Johnny grunted his approval.

"Where are we going?" Andi's heart thudded against the inside of her chest.

"You want to see your horse, don't you?" Johnny said. At Andi's mute nod, he barked, "Then shut up and do what I tell you." He indicated the sorrel horse. "Mount up."

Andi did what she was told. Her gaze was riveted on the creamy strands in Johnny's hand. How in the world had he gotten hold of her horse? She'd seen the wretched boy only an hour ago. He'd had no time to—

"Make room."

Johnny's rough orders cut into Andi's musing. He swung up behind her and squeezed into the saddle. It was an impossible fit. She might as well sit in his lap. She opened her mouth to complain, but Johnny whipped out a bandana.

"Hold still," he ordered when she twisted around to see what he was up to.

"What's that for?" she asked.

"You don't need to see where we're going."

Andi shot Jack a pleading look just before everything went dark. "Not so tight," she begged. The bandana's stench gagged her. *I can't do this!* If she hollered good and loud, *Help, I'm being kidnapped!* half of Fresno would come running.

Johnny and Jack had gone too far. This was criminal.

"Here." Johnny stuffed Taffy's mane into Andi's hand. "That's to remind you not to do anything stupid." He chuckled when Andi bristled. "I know you, Andi. You've got a notion to holler and bring the town running. But you won't get your horse back that way."

Andi lifted her hand to tear away the disgusting blindfold, but Johnny slapped it aside. "Take it easy. Just do what we say and everything will turn out fine."

Andi couldn't see where she was going, but she sensed they had wandered through back alleys and little-used side streets to leave

Fresno unnoticed. Once out of town, Johnny urged the horse into a lope. Andi heard Jack's horse following a few hoofbeats behind.

She tried to keep track of the passing time, but as the minutes wore on, she gave up. She didn't know where they were headed and she didn't care. All she wanted was to see Taffy, safe and sound.

A white-hot rage burned through her veins when she imagined Taffy's appearance—the rest of her mare's beautiful, creamy mane hacked and disfigured. Then a worse thought stabbed her. Would rough treatment harm the foal Taffy was carrying?

Angry tears soaked the blindfold. Her shoulders shook.

"What's the matter?" Johnny asked. "We're not going to hurt you. We just want to keep you out of town for a few days, until after the trial."

That dumb trial. She kept her mouth shut even though she wanted to scream her outrage.

If it weren't for Andi's desire to see Taffy, she'd rip the blindfold from her eyes, yank the reins, and make the horse rear. Johnny was clearly no horseman. Even at an easy lope his legs slapped against the horse's sides. It would be no trick for Andi to help him part company with the horse.

But when she fingered Taffy's mane, she settled back to wait. She could put up with Johnny as long as he led her to her beloved horse.

Walk, trot, lope. Walk, trot, lope. Andi felt like she had been smashed between the pommel of the saddle and Johnny for days, but it couldn't have been more than an hour or two. When he finally brought the horse to a stop, he yanked the bandana from Andi's eyes and dismounted.

Andi groaned in relief at being free from Johnny's sickening presence. She looked around. Dusk had settled on a small line shack nestled in the foothills. Scrub oak and pine, along with gently rolling hills, surrounded the cabin. It stood alone in the middle of thousands of acres of rangeland, a welcome shelter for cowhands working far from the home ranch. The last glow of sunset lingered in the west.

Andi slid from the horse and called, "Taffy!" Puckering her lips, she gave her special whistle.

Every nerve tingled while she listened for her mare's answering whicker. Andi didn't plan on staying here any longer than it took to mount Taffy and gallop away. She would not let Johnny and Jack carry out their lamebrain scheme to keep her from testifying.

Andi whistled again. Taffy didn't appear, and her heart skipped a beat. Where could her mare be? Had she gotten loose after Johnny brought her here? She could be anywhere . . . wherever *here* was.

She glanced around, hoping to recognize a familiar landmark. No use. The foothills all looked the same. And the hundreds of line shacks scattered throughout the Sierra foothills all looked alike. Andi had no idea where she was.

She planted her hands on her hips and faced Johnny. "All right. Where is she?"

Johnny walked up to Andi and grabbed her wrist. "Don't get all high and mighty. Let's go inside. We're going to be here awhile. Might as well get comfortable."

"Not until I see my horse." She tried to peel Johnny's fingers from her arm. "Let me go."

"I'll let you go once we're inside," he promised.

Andi whirled on Jack, who hadn't spoken a word since they'd left town. "Where's Taffy?"

Jack didn't answer. He didn't have to. Andi saw the truth in his face and gasped. "You don't have Taffy. You *lied* to me. Both of you!" Her fury spilled over, and she twisted free of Johnny.

But not for long.

"Come back here!" Johnny caught Andi in his arms before she reached the horses. With little effort, he lifted her up and carried her to the line shack.

Andi did not go quietly. Kicking and shrieking, she wriggled her arms free of his crushing grip. She lashed out at his head, grabbed two handfuls of hair, and yanked with all her might.

Johnny yelped, but he didn't let go. Once inside, he slammed Andi onto a rough bench next to the table and plunked himself down across from her. He leaned over the table and raised his fist. "Do it again, I dare you," he growled.

Jack sprang to Andi's side. He closed his hand around Johnny's arm and smashed it against the table. "Don't," he warned. "I mean it, Johnny. Don't touch her." He held the older boy's angry gaze until Johnny backed down with a shrug.

"I wasn't going to hit her. I only wanted to scare her." He shook free of Jack and rubbed his arm. "I didn't know you were sweet on her."

"I'm not," Jack replied icily. "I'm up to my neck in this now, but I want to stay clear of any *real* trouble."

"If that's your plan, Jack, then you better learn to think for yourself." Andi swiped her eyes with the back of her hand. Johnny and Jack would *not* see her cry. "Where's my horse?"

Johnny rose from the table, found a kerosene lamp, and lit it. After he'd turned up the flame, he set it down in front of Andi. "Taffy isn't the only palomino in Fresno County." He raised his fingers and made snipping motions in the air. "It's amazing how much horse hair a person can buy for a dollar. I know you love Taffy. It was easy to trick you into coming."

I knew he couldn't have stolen Taffy from the ranch. Andi kicked herself mentally. *I knew it. Why didn't I—*

"It took a bit more convincing to get Jack to go along," Johnny was saying. "But he's been eyeing those pearl-handled pistols over at Mason's Gun Shop."

Jack threw himself onto the line shack's one cot. "Shut up, Johnny." He put his hands behind his head and studied the ceiling.

Johnny stood and looked down at Andi. "Are you hungry?"

Food was the last thing on her mind. "No."

"You're going to be here awhile. I brought in a few supplies." He indicated one of the walls.

Andi glanced up. Although the lamp was blazing next to her, the rest of the cabin faded into darkness. She couldn't see the supplies. No matter. She couldn't eat. Her gaze flicked toward the door. If only—

"You take so much as one step toward that door and I'll tie you up," Johnny warned her.

Andi nodded. She was too scared to try another escape attempt. Not tonight. Instead, she spent the next half hour hunched over the table, wondering how Johnny and Jack hoped to get away with their scheme. They'd have to take her home sooner or later. When the truth came out, the boys would land in jail if Andi's family had any say.

The thought of the boys getting what they deserved should have cheered Andi, but her thoughts kept returning to Jack. His feeble warning had come too late. Was he having second thoughts since he'd talked to Peter? Maybe she could convince him to stand up to Johnny and take her home at first light.

The sound of approaching hoofbeats brought Andi's head up. *Now what?*

Johnny threw the door wide open. "It's my father."

"Your *father?*" Jack scrambled up from the cot. "What's he doing here?"

Andi's heart leaped. Mr. Wilson would bring a quick end to his bully son's behavior.

Charles Wilson strolled through the doorway. He spared his son a brief glance before turning his attention on Andi. "Good evening, Andrea."

She jumped up. "I'm mighty glad to see you, Mr. Wilson. Jack and Johnny have some fool plan to keep me from testifying on Tuesday. My mother must be worried sick. You'll take me home, won't you?"

Mr. Wilson motioned Andi to be quiet. He found a stool and lowered himself onto it. "Sit down, please. I'd like to talk to you."

Something in his voice sent chills up Andi's spine. She backed up and found her seat. "What the boys have done is against the law. If you don't take me home, you'll be breaking the law too."

Mr. Wilson sighed. "Believe me, Andrea, I know. And I'm sorry." He looked at Johnny. "I rode out to tell you I've changed my mind about keeping her here. It won't work. The judge will probably grant an extension until she's found, and we'll be right back where we started."

"But, Father," Johnny protested. "That wasn't the plan. You can't just let her go."

"Yes, I can." Mr. Wilson patted Andi on the knee. "I believe the best thing is for you to take the witness stand on Tuesday, after all."

Andi didn't know what to say. She looked at Jack, who sat frozen on the other side of the table. He looked like he wished he was anyplace else. She glanced at Johnny. He was fuming.

Mr. Wilson kept talking. "Let's see if we can straighten this whole thing out once and for all. You didn't see Peter kill anybody. There were too many shadows. You saw Ben Decker lying dead in the alley and a stranger running the other way. That's how it really happened, isn't it?"

Andi shook her head. "That's not true, Mr. Wilson. Peter told you what really happened."

"Nonsense. Peter is too distraught to think clearly." He took a deep breath. "You won't consider admitting that you made a mistake?"

"No, sir."

Mr. Wilson grunted. "All right then. Johnny will take you home at first light."

Johnny sputtered, but his father silenced him with a look.

Andi wanted to throw her arms around Mr. Wilson. "Thank you, sir," she said, smiling. *And thank you, God!*

The man continued as if Andi had not spoken. "You will go home and rest from this little ordeal my son and his friend put you through. Come Tuesday, you will take the stand and confess to your mistake. You will admit my son was nowhere near Ben that Friday afternoon." His voice hardened. "I don't care what you say—either you found the body or you saw somebody else do the killing—but you will leave Peter out of the entire affair."

Andi sat still, dazed at this sudden turn of events. It took her a full minute before she could answer. "No. I won't do that."

Mr. Wilson's dark gaze pierced her. "I think you will." He rose and crossed the room. When he reached the door, he sighed. "You are a stubborn young lady, and I am truly sorry it has come to this. I don't want to hurt you or your family, but you leave me no choice. Peter means more to me than anything in the world. More than our families' friendship. I don't intend to let him go to prison for a crime he didn't commit."

Johnny flinched at his father's words. Andi felt a spark of sympathy for him, but it was snuffed out at Mr. Wilson's next words.

"I took the liberty of gathering up something you are extremely fond of, to guarantee that you will keep your testimony exactly as I say. Everyone in this valley knows what stock you place in that horse of yours, and believe me, she *is* a beauty. It's easy to believe you love her more than you love most people."

"Johnny already tried that trick," Andi said.

"It's no trick. Not this time."

"You brought her horse?" Johnny's face showed his surprise. "What good does that do?"

"You'll see." Mr. Wilson opened the door a crack and beckoned Andi to join him.

The faint light spilling through the narrow opening revealed a golden palomino tied securely to the crude hitching post just outside the door. "For the right amount of money, it's possible to find someone willing to take a horse from *any* ranch—even yours."

Andi cried out and raced to Taffy. She threw her arms around her neck. Her mare seemed fine. Taffy nickered a happy greeting and nuzzled Andi's hair.

They hang horse thieves in California, she wanted to shriek. But no words came.

Mr. Wilson came up beside her. "No harm will come to your horse and the foal she's carrying," he promised. "You'll get her back so long as you do exactly as you're told." He ran his hand along Taffy's back. "If you don't follow instructions, you'll never see this horse again. Now, are you ready to settle down so we can take you home in the morning? Or are you going to fuss and carry on all night?"

Andi drew in a shaky breath and closed her eyes. *Forgive me, Lord,* she prayed. Then she opened her eyes. "You win, Mr. Wilson. I'll do whatever you ask."

Chapter Seventeen

ANDI'S SECRET

Johnny pulled his horse to a stop and removed the bandana from Andi's eyes. Dawn was a pale streak in the sky. "We're about a half mile from your ranch. You can walk the rest of the way."

Andi slid from the horse with a weary sigh. It had been another long, uncomfortable ride wedged between Johnny and the pommel of his saddle. She was certain he took great delight in knowing how she hated being close to him.

Johnny chuckled. "Yes, Miss Carter, it's been a real pleasure escorting you home."

Andi sagged against the horse. "Go away, Johnny. You've tormented me enough for one night."

"Sure. But don't forget that Jack's watching your horse. You better do like my father says, or else."

Andi pushed away from the horse and glared up at Johnny. It was clear he'd quickly adjusted to his father's change of plans. So had Jack. Although, Andi mused, Jack had looked scared out of his wits when he agreed to stay at the cabin with Taffy.

If I only knew where she was being kept! But the blindfold had done its work well. "You're a beast!"

"I like you too." Johnny blew her a kiss. "See you in court." He jammed his heels into his horse and trotted away.

Andi groaned. The instructions for her new testimony seared her tired mind. On Tuesday, in front of everyone, she would tell the "real" story. Then she would confess that she'd made up her first testimony because she wanted revenge against Johnny.

Andi's face burned. She would be shamed before the whole town, and her family would be disgraced right along with her.

Mr. Wilson's final orders had been even harder to bear. She could not tell her family where she'd been or with whom she'd spoken. She must say she'd run off to be by herself.

Andi didn't want to imagine her mother's reaction to *that*. For an instant she considered running away for real, at least until the trial was over.

But that would not save Taffy.

She's just a horse, a voice in her head insisted. *But Taffy's more than a horse*, a second voice argued. *She's my friend. I can't betray her, even if she is only an animal.*

The internal battle raged until Andi reached the ranch house. Miraculously, the yard was empty. She darted to the kitchen entrance and opened the door. Slipping inside, she tiptoed toward the back stairs.

"Andi!" Rosa flung aside her dish towel, dashed across the kitchen, and gave Andi a bone-crushing embrace. "What happened to you? Everyone is worried." She started crying. "I told *Señor* Justin you worked at the mercantile. Forgive me for giving away your secret. I did not know what else to do. *Señor* Justin kept asking and asking. He looked so upset that I finally told him."

Andi caught her breath. "What did he say?"

"He said nothing. He thanked me and left. It was very late, but I think he went to town." Her eyebrows came together in a frown. *"¿Qué pasó, amiga?"*

"I can't tell you what happened. I can't tell anyone. It's—"

"Where in blazes have you been?" Chad's bellow made both girls jump. He stood in the dining room doorway, hands on hips, glaring at his sister. "Do you have any idea how worried we've been?

Mother's beside herself. I've got every ranch hand out searching for you."

Andi bit her lip, unable to repeat the story Mr. Wilson had given her. She couldn't lie to her brother. She couldn't tell him the truth either. She was stuck. *Best not to say anything at all.*

Rosa squeezed Andi's hand and scurried away.

Andi didn't blame her for leaving. Not many folks stood up to Chad. Andi wasn't afraid to face her bossy older brother most days, but this morning her head was aching. Why couldn't he leave her alone? She started up the back stairs.

Chad hurried over and caught her sleeve. "Answer me."

Andi yanked free and backed against the stairwell wall. "I *won't* tell you. I'm tired. I'm tired of worrying about the trial, I'm tired of being gossiped about, and I'm tired of your bossing. I'm going to bed." *Stay angry! Then you won't cry.*

It was no use. The tears she had held back since last night spilled over.

Neither Andi's words nor her tears moved Chad. He looked too worn-out and frustrated to care. "Listen here, little sister. You kept us up all night. We deserve an explanation."

"Don't force her," Justin interrupted. He walked around the table and clapped a hand on his brother's shoulder. "Take it easy, Chad. Mother will get to the bottom of this in her own way." He gave Andi a tired smile. "Go up to bed, honey. I'll tell Mother you're safe."

Andi clattered up the stairs without looking back.

She had no sooner peeled off her dress, thrown her nightgown over her head, and curled up under her bedcovers when she heard a rap on her door. There was no time to respond. Someone opened the door and stepped into the room. "Andrea, what is going on?"

Andi peeked through mostly closed eyelids. A mixture of disappointment, worry, and annoyance showed on her mother's face. *This is not going to be easy. Maybe if I pretend I'm asleep she'll go away.*

Andi waited, but her mother did not leave. She looked ready to stand next to the bed all morning for an answer. "I'm sorry I worried you," Andi finally murmured. "It won't happen again."

"I dare say it won't." Mother sat down on the edge of the bed. "Where were you?"

"Just . . . around." That much was true.

Andi felt a gentle hand stroke her hair. "I'm afraid I can't accept that answer, sweetheart. Your disappearance from town yesterday afternoon frightened us more than anything else that's happened these past few weeks. Then you turn up this morning with no explanation. You didn't wander off and get lost. Of that I'm certain."

Andi pulled the covers over her head. She couldn't answer. Instead she complained, "Can't I keep anything to myself around here?"

"Not when it affects the entire family," Mother replied. "Chad's especially upset. Not only did you disappear, but he also discovered that Taffy's not in her stall. Do you know where she is?"

"She's . . . she's . . ." Andi struggled to think of a truthful answer to the question.

"Out on the range?"

"Yes." Taffy was indeed on the range, just probably not on Carter rangeland.

"I see." Mother rose from the bed. "Andrea, look at me."

Andi pushed the covers away, swept her hair off her forehead, and met her mother's soft blue gaze. "I'm fine," she said in a small voice. "Just worn out."

"Justin believes you've stumbled into some kind of trouble— something having to do with the trial on Tuesday. He'd like to talk to you."

Andi winced. She didn't dare talk to Justin. He had the uncanny ability of finding out from Andi anything he wished to know. Sometimes he even figured things out by what she *didn't* say. No, being questioned by Justin was not a good idea.

He's probably talked to Mr. Goodwin by now and knows all about my working there. What else does he suspect?

She shook her head. "I don't want to talk to Justin right now."

"Perhaps you'll change your mind after a good, long nap."

I can't, Andi thought.

"In the meantime, you may not leave the ranch until after the trial," her mother continued. "No trips to town, no school on Monday. You'll stay indoors, where I can keep an eye on you." She sighed. "I'm frightened. Since you refuse to tell me the trouble, I can't help you. The only way I can protect you is by keeping you nearby."

"Yes, ma'am," Andi whispered.

Mother bent down, planted a kiss on her forehead, and left the room.

Andi rolled over and fell asleep.

"Today's the day," Chad announced when Andi sat down for breakfast Tuesday morning. "You ready for the trial?"

Andi answered with a shrug. She flooded her oatmeal with cream and tried to eat the gummy mess. After one bite, she shuddered and pushed the bowl away.

"Cheer up, Andi. After today everything will be back to normal around here." Chad poured himself a cup of coffee. "And I say it's about time. I've had enough of this trial business to last me a year."

"Amen to that," Mitch agreed. He grinned at Andi. "Don't worry, Sis. You won't be going into that courthouse alone. We'll be right there."

Swell, Andi mourned silently. *You can all watch me make a fool of myself on the witness stand.* She bowed her head and stared at the remains of her oatmeal. "I don't feel very well."

"You'll feel better once it's over," Justin told her. To Andi's relief, he had given up trying to talk to her about her disappearance. "Answer the questions truthfully and you'll be fine," he continued.

"We've prayed about it. We've gone over your testimony a dozen times. Don't be afraid of Peter's lawyer. He'll try to confuse you and make you say things that cast doubt on what you saw. But don't worry. You're ready to do this."

Andi nodded, but she didn't look up. Justin could counsel her until he was blue in the face, but Andi had already been taught her lines. At the trial, she would buy Taffy back with a lie.

Chapter Eighteen

THE TRIAL

The courthouse was packed to overflowing. People chatted freely, laughing and jostling each other for the best places to sit. Peter Wilson's trial was clearly the entertainment of the year. Andi and her family had ringside seats near the front of the courtroom. She sat down at the end of the row, next to Justin, and stared at the empty witness chair with fear and trembling.

The clamor grew louder. Andi turned around to watch. She rested her chin on her arms and leaned over the back of her seat, gazing curiously at the noisy spectators. She recognized cowboys and businessmen, elderly matrons and saloon girls. Her stomach tightened when she saw Megan and Robbie Decker enter and take seats near the back.

Megan nodded. Robbie smiled and waved.

Andi didn't acknowledge their greetings.

Her gaze moved to the defendant's table. Peter sat quietly, his expression downcast. His lawyer spoke to him, and Peter shrugged.

He sure doesn't look happy, Andi thought. *He looks like I feel.*

All too soon, a loud voice announced, "All rise for the honorable Judge Samuel Morrison." A hush fell over the crowd. The trial was about to begin.

The first order of business was selecting a jury. Sometimes it took an hour. Sometimes it took days. Each lawyer wanted jurors sympathetic to his side of the case. To pass the time, Andi counted flies.

Plenty of them buzzed around the courtroom on this warm autumn day. Counting flies was a way Andi could avoid thinking about what would happen next.

The jury selection dragged into mid morning. Finally, the prosecution and the defense lawyers announced they were satisfied.

"It's about time," Andi muttered, which earned her a sharp glance from Justin. She sighed and slumped in her seat.

Once they had agreed on the twelve men who would decide Peter's fate, the two lawyers took turns delivering their opening statements to the jury. It seemed silly. Everybody in town already knew both sides of the case. Why did Mr. Powers and Mr. Browning have to present it all over again?

Andi yawned. Would they never stop talking?

Beside her, Justin appeared absorbed in the proceedings. A frown creased his brow. Andi peered down the row at the rest of her family. They were listening with the same intensity as Justin.

This is worse than listening to Mr. Foster drone on and on about the long-dead emperors of China. She leaned wearily against her brother and whispered, "What's taking so long?"

Justin shushed her.

Sighing, Andi hunched over, propped her elbows on her knees, and rested her head in her hands. Fear washed over her in waves. If only she didn't have to go up there. If only something would happen to interrupt the proceedings.

Her imagination came alive. *What about an earthquake? Or a fire? Or maybe someone will run in and yell that the bank's being robbed. Better still, maybe a—*

"The state of California calls Miss Andrea Carter to the stand."

Andi jerked to attention. Her mouth went dry and her heart skipped a beat. She felt glued in place.

A nudge brought her out of her daze. "Go on, honey." Justin's voice was a whisper in her ear. "You've done this before. It should come easy this time around."

With her heart in her throat, Andi stood. Her legs felt like jelly. She certainly hadn't felt this way during the inquest. She'd been uneasy, but nothing like what she was feeling now. The thought of lying in front of all these people . . .

She swallowed. *The truth will set you free*, a calm voice whispered in her head. She pushed the gentle prodding aside, wiped her clammy hands against her skirt, and made her way to the front.

Matthew Powers, the district attorney, smiled at her when she passed by.

She didn't return his smile. *You won't be smiling after you hear my testimony*, she thought dismally. *You'll be so shocked you'll probably fall down dead.*

Guilt stabbed her. Matt Powers was Justin's friend. He'd been especially kind to her during the inquest and all the other times she'd talked with him during the past few weeks. She hated what she had to do.

Andi slipped into the witness chair and looked at the man towering above her from the judge's bench. Judge Morrison peered at Andi over his spectacles and gave her a half-smile. His smile did nothing to calm her nerves. Justin had explained that Judge Morrison wasn't too keen on children testifying.

Would Judge Morrison throw her in jail if he discovered she wasn't telling the truth?

The court clerk brought a Bible over so she could be sworn in. "Raise your right hand." Andi obeyed. "Do you solemnly swear to tell the truth, the whole truth, and nothing but the truth, so help you God?"

Andi stared at the big, black book under her sweaty palm. *How can I promise to tell the truth and then not do it?* She heard a rustling from the bench and looked up.

Judge Morrison leaned his elbow on the bench and rested a fleshy cheek against his palm. "Miss Carter, you cannot testify until you are sworn in. Are you going to do that any time soon?"

Andi flushed. She turned to the young man holding the Bible. "I do." She wondered if God would strike her dead.

The judge let out a breath. "Thank you." He looked at the district attorney. "Proceed, Counselor."

Matthew Powers approached the witness stand and gave Andi a friendly smile. "It's a little frightening to be sitting up here with so many people looking at you, isn't it?"

What a dumb question! Andi would sooner face a wild stallion than the people staring at her from the spectator seats. But she knew Mr. Powers was doing his best to make her feel comfortable, so she nodded.

"There's no reason to be afraid," he continued. "I'm going to ask you a few questions, ones I've asked you before. When I'm finished, Mr. Browning will ask you some questions. Then you can sit down. All right?"

At the mention of Peter's lawyer, Andi turned her attention to the defense table. Mr. Browning was studying her with cold, cunning eyes. He looked like a hawk ready to swoop down on a helpless bunny. Justin had warned her that Mr. Browning would not be kind.

"Andi?"

She pulled her gaze back to Mr. Powers and nodded.

"First of all, I want you to tell the court where you were on the afternoon of Friday, September sixteenth, between the hours of four and five o'clock."

"Over in the warehouse district, in an alley." So far, so good.

"What were you doing there?"

Andi relaxed. These were easy questions. "Following a puppy."

"Why?"

"He had a hurt foot. I wanted to help."

Mr. Powers smiled at her. "Were you able to catch the dog?"

"Yes, sir. I caught him and pulled a big thorn from his paw."

Peter's lawyer stood. "Objection, Your Honor. This is all very interesting, but the details surrounding this poor, unfortunate animal are not relevant." He smiled. "Unless the dog is a witness too?"

A murmur of laughter rippled through the courtroom.

Judge Morrison sighed. "Sustained. Move on, Mr. Powers."

Mr. Powers nodded. "What happened after you relieved the puppy of its misery, Andi?"

"I heard a yell, and a door slammed."

"What did you do?"

"I hid. I was scared."

Andi grew more and more uncomfortable as Mr. Powers made her remember everything in vivid detail. She told how she had seen two men fighting and how, after being pushed, the victim had fallen down the stairs to his death.

The crowd hung on every word.

"Did you recognize the victim?"

"Not at first," Andi said. "I ran away. But when I saw him the second time—when Justin took me back to the alley—I learned it was Ben Decker."

Mr. Powers gave Andi a pleased smile. "You're doing fine. I have only a few more questions, to make sure everything is perfectly clear."

Andi laced her fingers together in her lap and waited. *Here it comes.*

"You testified that from your hiding place in the shadows you saw two men fighting, correct?"

Andi nodded.

"Please answer the question aloud so the court reporter can take down what you say," Mr. Powers said.

"That's right."

"You also told us that during the fight, it looked like one man pushed the other so that he fell down the stairs. The man who fell was Ben Decker, correct?

"Yes."

"Did you recognize the other man involved in the fight? The man who pushed Ben Decker?"

Andi shifted uncomfortably in her seat. She saw Johnny, and her throat tightened. He sat in the first row of spectator seats, stone-faced and dressed in his best. She swallowed.

"Andi?"

She dropped her gaze to her lap and said nothing.

The crowd began to murmur. The judge tapped his gavel. "There will be order in this courtroom. Please answer the question, Miss Carter."

"It . . . it . . . was dark," she whispered, raising her head.

Mr. Powers stared at her, mouth agape. He took a deep breath then let it out. "Perhaps you misunderstood the question," he suggested. "Let me ask it another way. Did you see a man fighting with Ben Decker?"

Andi had already answered that question when she explained she'd seen two men fighting. "Yes," she admitted, "I saw him."

"Did he push Ben down the stairs?"

"Yes."

"Is the man you saw sitting in this courtroom?"

Andi looked down. She clasped her hands tightly together and squeezed her eyes shut. *Tell him!* Her conscience screamed at her. *The truth will set you free!*

The sound of the gavel banging jolted Andi from her troubled thoughts. The judge's eyes blazed. "Answer the question, young lady."

"I . . . I don't know."

Andi was unprepared for the effect her words had on the courtroom. Shocked expressions and gasps came from the spectators. Maxwell Browning leaned back in his chair and steepled his fingers under his chin. Charles Wilson's face was wreathed in smiles. Johnny looked ready to leap for joy.

But Peter's face was chalk-white.

Within seconds, the courtroom burst into noisy speculation.

"Order!" Judge Morrison banged his gavel. "I will have order." He pointed the gavel at Matthew Powers. "Proceed, Counselor."

Mr. Powers was clearly caught off guard. He exchanged an astonished look with Justin, who stared at Andi. *What do you think you're doing?* was etched on her brother's features—from his furrowed forehead and the grim set of his mouth to the barely perceptible shake of his head.

Andi read it all in a second and nearly burst into tears.

With a nod to the judge, Mr. Powers returned to his suddenly uncooperative witness. When he spoke, his voice was harsh with dismay. "What do you mean, *you don't know*? You were certain of what you saw when questioned at the inquest, and when questioned numerous times since."

Andi blinked back tears and sought a friendly face in the first row. Her mother smiled and gave her a slight nod.

The truth will set you free, the quiet voice insisted. But it wouldn't set Taffy free. She couldn't tell Mr. Powers the truth. She clamped her jaw shut. *Nobody can make me talk. Nobody!*

Justin rose from his seat. "Your Honor, if you would grant a short recess, perhaps we could—"

"You're out of order, Mr. Carter," the judge said. "I don't believe you are representing anyone here today. Sit down, sir."

Chad leaped to his feet. "Don't jump all over him, Judge. He's only concerned about Andi. Something strange is going on. Let Justin talk to her."

"Objection!" Maxwell Browning called out.

"Enough of this!" Judge Morrison slammed the gavel onto his bench with a deafening *crash*. "Sit down, Mr. Carter, or I will have you removed."

Chad sat, bristling.

Andi wanted to sink through the floor.

Judge Morrison gestured to Mr. Powers. "If you would bring this portion of the proceedings to a close, I'd appreciate it." He glared at Andi. "And no more foolishness from *you* either, Miss Carter."

Mr. Powers looked at Andi. "I don't know what's going on here, but I'm going to ask this question one more time. I want you to answer yes or no. Can you identify the man who pushed Ben Decker down the steps?"

Andi felt sick—sicker than at any other time of her life. Why couldn't she simply say "no" and be done with it? Peter would go free and she'd get Taffy back. Nobody in this courtroom cared that Ben Decker was dead—not even his son and daughter.

Maybe God didn't care either.

The truth will set you free! Trust Me! The voice shouted in her head.

The world began to spin. Andi's hands grew clammy. Her heart pounded against the inside of her chest like galloping hooves. She blinked, and Mr. Powers's face blurred. His voice seemed to come from inside a long, dark tunnel. "Yes or no, Andrea," he kept insisting. "Answer the question."

Andi closed her eyes to steady herself. It was the last thing she remembered.

Chapter Nineteen

SURPRISE WITNESS

"It looks like you got your recess after all, Justin."

Andi roused at the sound of Matthew Powers's voice. She was lying on a settee in the judge's chambers, surrounded by her family.

"Are you all right, sweetheart?" Mother placed a cool hand on Andi's forehead.

"What happened?" Andi sat up and looked around. "How did I get here?"

Justin joined their mother on the sofa. "You fainted. You tumbled right off the witness stand and into Matt's arms." He chuckled. "It caused quite a stir. Even Judge Morrison looked worried." His smile faded. "You may rest for a few minutes, but then you have to go back and answer the question."

Andi clenched her jaw. "I can't."

"You must," Mother insisted. "I don't know what the trouble is, but you *must* testify."

"I think I know," Justin said. "You didn't spend Friday night alone, did you? Someone took you away and pressured you to change your story." He leaned closer. "What did they say? How did they threaten you?" When Andi didn't answer, Justin pleaded, "You *have* to tell us, honey."

Andi burst into tears. As usual, Justin had figured out most of it. In a rush of words, she told her family about Taffy. "So you see," she finished weakly, "I *have* to do what Mr. Wilson told me or I'll never see Taffy again."

She wiped her eyes with a handkerchief her mother handed her. "But when I got up on the witness stand, I couldn't do it. Oh, Mother! I tried, but I couldn't *lie*. So I said as little as possible. That didn't work either. Now Mr. Wilson knows you're talking with me and he'll . . . he'll . . ." Her voice trailed off in misery. She would never see Taffy again.

Chad clenched his fists. "Of all the miserable, low-down—"

Mother silenced him with a look.

"What am I going to do?" Andi searched her mother's face for an answer.

"Listen to me, Andrea," Mother said. "You must take the stand and tell the truth about Peter. If you don't, you'll never be free. Your conscience will give you no peace." She took Andi's hands and squeezed them. "Believe me, sweetheart, *nothing* is more precious than a clear conscience before God."

The truth will set you free. Her mother's words echoed Andi's thoughts. "What about Taffy?"

"It won't be easy, but you'll have to let God take care of Taffy. *You* are going to tell the truth, even if you're afraid. We'll do our best to find Taffy."

"You can count on that," Mitch said.

Mother guided Andi off the settee. Then she wrapped her arms around her daughter and kissed her forehead. "I want you to go out there and show Charles Wilson and his attorney that he can't scare a Carter out of telling the truth."

A few minutes later, the call came. Andi marched to the front of the courtroom and took her seat with grim determination. She risked a quick peek at the defense table. Peter's lawyer was no longer smiling.

Matthew Powers stood beside the witness chair. "Did you see who pushed Ben Decker?"

"Yes, I did." In spite of her quivering insides, Andi's voice rang out loud and clear in the still courtroom. "It was Peter Wilson." A huge burden fell from her shoulders. She felt weak with relief. *Mother was right.*

Mr. Wilson's palm slammed down against the railing. "No!"

Before Judge Morrison could silence him, the door to the courtroom banged open. Jack Goodwin ran in, disheveled and breathless. He looked around wildly until his gaze fell on Andi in the witness chair. Ignoring the whispers and surprised looks, he hurried up the aisle.

"What is the meaning of this interruption?" the judge bellowed. "Who are you?"

"Jack Goodwin, sir. Has Andi testified?"

"She's testifying right now." The judge frowned. "Now clear out. This is a court of law, boy, not a church social."

"I'm sorry, Your Honor," Jack said, "but there's something Andi needs to know right away." He looked at her. "You don't have to worry about Taffy. She's right outside. I rode her in a few minutes ago."

Andi gaped at Jack. Taffy, here? Safe? *Oh, God, You knew all along. Thank you!*

"The longer I sat up at the line shack, the more I started thinking for myself," Jack said. "It didn't make sense that Mr. Wilson would threaten you with your horse if Peter truly was innocent." He spread his hands wide. "I hope I'm not too late. It took time to make up my mind. Now you can tell the truth without worrying about your horse."

The courtroom exploded into a noisy mob. Not even Judge Morrison's gavel could bring the crowd to order. Charles Wilson buried his head in his hands. His shoulders slumped in defeat. Peter's lawyer exchanged a few quick words with his young client, and then gathered up his books and notes. He rose and left the courtroom.

When the commotion finally died down, Judge Morrison excused

Andi. She jumped down and hurried to Jack. "Thank you," she whispered in his ear. "That's the nicest thing anybody ever did for me."

Jack swallowed. "I . . . I . . . You're welcome."

Mr. Goodwin pushed his way through the crowd and grabbed Jack by the shoulders. "You worried me sick, boy," he scolded. "Gone all night without a trace." Then his frown turned to a wide grin. "But right now I'm mighty proud of you."

"Your Honor?" A shaky voice drew everyone's attention to the defense table, where Peter Wilson stood. His face was pale, but he held his head high. "I'd like to change my plea to 'guilty.' I *was* fighting with Ben Decker, just like Andi testified at the inquest. I caused his death. He was blackmailing me. Demanding money to keep quiet about my seeing his daughter, Megan."

The spectators hung on Peter's every word. Not a skirt rustled. No one coughed.

Peter turned red. "I told Ben I wouldn't pay him another cent. He got rough with me, and I fought back. He was drunk, angry, and seemed intent on killing me. I pushed him away and he fell down the stairs. When I saw he was dead, and I saw Andi standing there, I panicked. I should have stayed and told the sheriff the truth, but I didn't want my family to know about Megan." His shoulders slumped. "I'm so ashamed."

Andi listened to Peter's confession with mixed feelings. She was glad he had admitted his guilt, but she hurt for Megan. It wasn't fair that folks looked down on her because of her father's reputation.

Peter lifted his gaze to the packed courtroom and scanned the crowd. From where she stood, Andi had a clear view of Megan and Robbie in the back row. The young woman held her head high in spite of Peter's hurtful words. "I'm sorry, Megan. I have wronged you. If I'd been honest and open from the beginning, your father would still be alive." His voice shook. "My father would have been scandalized, but not any more than he is now, by what *he* has done. Forcing Andi to change her story . . ."

He cleared his throat. "Please forgive me, Megan, for being a coward and not standing up to my family on your account. I've been a fool and have hurt a lot of people."

When Megan nodded, Peter slumped back into his seat and let out a long, heartfelt sigh. "Thank you." He sounded as if a huge burden had fallen from him.

Andi noticed it right away. She and Peter exchanged understanding looks. The truth had set *him* free too.

The judge shook his head. "This is most irregular." He banged his gavel for attention. "Since the defendant has changed his plea, I declare these proceedings a mistrial. Peter Wilson's case will be reviewed at a later date."

Andi waited for the judge to end the trial and tell everybody to go home, but he didn't. Instead, he narrowed his eyes and pierced Mr. Wilson with a hard look. "Charles Wilson, if there is any truth in what young Jack Goodwin has told us, then you will be facing your own set of charges very soon."

Mr. Wilson paled. "Yes, Your Honor."

Judge Morrison banged his gavel one more time. "Court is adjourned."

Chapter Twenty

THE PRICE OF A GIFT

"That's a beautiful shiner you've got, Jack. What happened?" Andi asked after school the next day. She gathered up her books and lunch pail and waited for Rosa to put away her things.

"He—" Cory began.

"I'll tell this myself," Jack interrupted. The shadow of a smile crept over his face. "Johnny didn't think much of what I did yesterday on your account. He called me a 'dirty traitor' and punched me in the face." He touched his swollen eye and winced. "I reckon we're not friends any longer."

"I reckon not," Andi said with a laugh. "I'm glad."

Cory clambered down the stairs. "And the best news?" he called over his shoulder. "Tell Jack what you told me, Andi, about Johnny and his father."

Andi rolled her eyes. "Nothing's on paper yet, but Justin came home last night after a meeting in the judge's chambers. Judge Morrison plans to order Mr. Wilson to choose between jail time and military school back east for Johnny."

"It's probably best if Johnny stays away from Fresno for a while," Cory said. "Folks are heated up over what he and his father tried to do to you."

Jack gave Andi a sheepish look as they left the schoolhouse. "I'm glad I came to my senses, or I'd probably be on the train with

Johnny—or worse." He gulped. "Maybe even jail. Do you suppose Mr. Wilson will go to jail for what he did?"

Andi wasn't sure. True, he'd had his hand in kidnapping her, and he'd obstructed justice by threatening a witness, and . . . "I can't remember everything Justin said, but he's certain Mr. Wilson will not get off scot-free. Judge Morrison made it clear that he would be punished."

She didn't repeat what Chad had said last night. "If Charles Wilson somehow escapes justice, I'll make sure the banker gets a taste of *Carter* justice."

Andi was never sure when Chad was just sounding off. She sure hoped he was this time. *I want to forget all of this as fast as I can.*

"Say, Andi," Jack said. "I didn't get a chance to apologize yesterday."

Andi grinned. "I would say bringing Taffy back is a mighty fine apology."

Jack shuffled his feet in the dust of the schoolyard. "All right. But there's more. You were right. Johnny's no good. I'm glad to be rid of him." He took a deep breath. "You helped me figure that out." He broke away from the group. "See you later. I've got deliveries to make for Pa." He headed down the street, whistling off-key.

Jack's decision to bring Taffy back had changed him. He'd become a hero overnight—at least to Andi—and his whole attitude about himself seemed better. Mr. Goodwin's pride in his son's decision also added to Jack's cheerfulness. Andi hoped it would last.

She told Cory good-bye and grabbed Rosa's hand to hurry her along. When the girls arrived at Justin's office, he was already outside, sitting in the buggy.

"Ah, there you are, ladies. I was just about to come looking for you. Hop in."

"What's the hurry?" Andi asked as she and Rosa climbed into the buggy. "Don't you have to work late?"

Justin laughed. "Not today. Have you forgotten it's Mother's birthday?" He pointed at a large, flat, rectangular bundle tied to the back of the rig. "There's the gift. Shall I include your name on it, like always?"

Andi stared at Justin in shock and dismay. How could she have forgotten Mother's birthday? The kidnapping, the crazy weekend, the trial, the confusion . . . *Well, I guess it's no wonder I didn't remember.*

"What's the matter?" Justin asked her. "You look like you've seen a ghost."

She didn't answer his question. "I've got to run over to Goodwin's for a minute. I'll be right back." Before Justin or Rosa could stop her, she leaped from the buggy and landed in the street at a run.

She entered the mercantile out of breath. In her haste, she nearly knocked over the cracker barrel. "Mr. Goodwin!"

"This is a nice surprise." Mr. Goodwin came out from behind the counter. "What's the trouble?"

"My music box. I left it here last Friday. Mother wouldn't let me come to town until the trial yesterday and then today"—she swallowed and tried to catch her breath—"I just remembered today's her birthday. May I have it?"

Mr. Goodwin looked puzzled. "I'm sorry, Andi, but I haven't seen the music box since you paid for it last Friday. You took it and left."

Andi bit her lip. The memory of last Friday slowly returned. "You're right. I had it when I went into the stockroom to put my apron in the bin. I set it down on a barrel." She raced past the shopkeeper and barged into the back room. Her gaze flew to the top of the barrel.

No music box.

"If you laid it on the barrel, I would have seen it," Mr. Goodwin told her.

"Will you help me look for it? I know I left it back here. Maybe it fell off when you were moving things around. It's *got* to be here."

Mr. Goodwin and Andi scoured the room for the missing item.

They searched behind barrels, under boxes, and in corners. Andi shoved canned goods out of the way and peered at the backs of shelves, but the music box was gone.

"Maybe Jack knows where it is," Andi suggested in a desperate voice.

"That could be, but Jack's not here. He's delivering three different orders all over town. When he returns, I'll ask him. Why don't you check back tomorrow?" Mr. Goodwin smiled at her disappointed look. "It'll turn up."

Tomorrow. Andi's shoulders slumped. Tomorrow would be too late.

"Don't fret, Andi. Your mother will love the gift even if it's a day late."

Andi knew Mr. Goodwin was trying to cheer her up, but it was no use. "I reckon there's nothing more I can do today." She shrugged. "Thanks for the help."

"I'm sorry," he said. "Tomorrow—"

"I'll come by in the morning. Good-bye."

Andi trudged back to the buggy and climbed in next to her brother.

"What was that all about?" Justin asked. He chirruped at the horse, and they started on their way. "You lit out of the buggy like it was on fire. If you'd waited half a second, I'd have given you a ride to the mercantile."

Andi grunted. She didn't feel much like talking.

Rosa reached across Justin's lap and squeezed Andi's hand. *"Todo estará bien,"* she whispered.

Andi wasn't sure everything would be all right, but she knew she had to put on a good face for Mother's sake. "What did you say about that gift back there?" she asked Justin, jerking her thumb behind her shoulder.

"I asked if you want your name on it."

"What is it?"

"A painting."

Andi wrinkled her nose. "A painting of what?"

"I think it's a painting of a buffalo hunt." At Andi's astonished look, Justin chuckled. "It was Chad's idea. He found it at a gallery in San Francisco last month and had it shipped here. It arrived just in time. He says Mother will love it."

Andi made a face. "Mother will love a picture of a *buffalo hunt?*"

Rosa giggled. Andi would have joined her if she hadn't felt so miserable about her own lack of a gift.

"Chad says a painting by George Catlin will be worth a lot of money someday," Justin explained. "Besides, he liked it."

"That's what you get for letting Chad pick out the gift," Andi muttered. More than ever she wished she had her music box to offer.

"I won't put your name on it if you have something else in mind." He looked at her long and hard. "Do you?"

"No. Go ahead and add it—like always." She rolled her eyes and sighed. *A buffalo hunt!*

Unshed tears blurred her vision. The surprise Andi had planned for her mother's birthday was ruined. She'd gone to town when she should have stayed home. She'd listened to hurtful gossip. She'd been kidnapped and her horse held hostage. All because she'd wanted to earn her precious gift in time.

All for nothing. She had failed in her determination to make this year different and special.

She felt empty.

Andi tried her best to keep a cheerful attitude. She complimented Melinda on the two-layer, pink-and-white birthday cake she'd made. It held so many candles that Andi was afraid they might burn the house down when they were lit. She hugged Mother and wished her a happy birthday.

When her brothers lifted the paper-wrapped gift and presented it to their mother, Andi moved away and sat on a footstool across the room. A pang stabbed her. *A picture of a buffalo hunt,* she thought gloomily. *I wish my name wasn't on it.* She wondered if Mother would notice the disappointment Andi was trying to hide.

Mother carefully tore the paper wrapping from the gilded frame. Her eyes widened when the painting appeared. "It's lovely," she said with a smile. "A George Catlin painting." She scanned the parlor for an empty spot on the wall. "I know just where I'd like to hang it. Thank you all very much. Whose idea was this?"

"Chad's," Justin and Mitch said together.

Chad grinned. "It's true I thought of it. But everybody had a part in making your birthday special this year, Mother."

"It's wonderful." She smiled at Andi. "What about you, Andrea? What was your part in this venture?"

Andi looked at the floor. "Not much. I—"

A loud knock at the door interrupted her confession. Luisa entered the room. "It is for *Señorita* Andrea," the housekeeper said.

Andi jumped up and ran for the door, grateful for the interruption. Jack stood on the porch, panting. His red cheeks and tousled hair gave away the fact that he'd pushed his horse to a gallop to get here.

Her heart raced. "Good grief, Jack. What's wrong? Why—"

"Here." He thrust a cloth-wrapped bundle at her. "I'm sorry, Andi. Pa told me you stopped by. I'd forgotten all about this thing. I hid it away before I joined you and Johnny with the horses last Friday. If Pa found it, he'd have known something was wrong. I meant to dig it out and give it to you at school, but I forgot. I hope it's not too late." He paused. "Is it?"

Andi clutched the small package in her hands. Her heart slowed to normal. Nothing was wrong. Everything was all right. A smile spread across her face. She hardly knew how to thank him for riding an hour out of his way to bring her the music box.

"It's not too late for your mother's party, is it?" Jack persisted.

"No." She reached out and took his hand. "You're just in time. Come on in."

Jack backed away. "I can't. Look at you. You're slicked up fancy, and I'm sweaty and in work clothes."

"Nobody'll care. Honest."

"Pa's expecting me right back. I really can't stay." He let go of Andi's hand and started for his horse.

"Jack," Andi called. He turned. Before she could change her mind, she stepped forward and gave him a quick peck on his cheek. "Thank you for bringing my music box back, and"—she grinned at the shocked look on his face—"thank you again for saving Taffy."

Jack's hand flew to his cheek. "It was n-nothing," he stuttered, flushing. He mounted his horse and gave it a hard nudge. "See you in school."

Andi closed the door. She returned to the parlor with her hands hidden behind her back.

"Who was here?" Melinda asked.

"Jack Goodwin."

"You didn't invite him to stay?"

"I did, but he had to get back to town." She brought the bundle from behind her back and set it in her mother's lap. "I'm sorry it's not properly wrapped."

Mother looked surprised. "What is it?"

Andi's heart overflowed with joy. "My birthday present to you."

"But . . ." She nodded at the painting.

Andi rolled her eyes. "The fancy art is from *them*. This is from *me*." She joined her on the settee. "Open it!"

The family crowded around to watch their mother open Andi's gift. When the last of the cloth wrappings fell away, Mother gasped. "Andrea, this is exquisite! I've never seen such a beautiful music box."

The look on her mother's face was everything Andi had hoped for. "Happy birthday, Mother." She hugged her tight. "I wanted to give you something I earned myself, something that would be only from me. I didn't want to ask anyone for the money."

"But, Andi!" Melinda took the music box and lifted the lid. "Brahms' Lullaby" tinkled merrily. "Where did you get the money? This must have cost—"

"This music box cost more than any of you realize," Justin said. He nodded at Andi's questioning look. "I found out what you were doing."

Of course. Friday night, when he searched Fresno. "At least you kept it to yourself," she said.

He smiled. "If you hadn't disappeared, I'd never have found out. You did a nice job keeping it a surprise. But when we couldn't find you, I pestered Rosa until she told me what you'd been up to."

"Poor Rosa," Andi said. Justin could be mighty insistent.

He winced. "Yes, but she was worried too. Andi worked at the mercantile every day after school to pay for the music box," he continued. "Paul Goodwin told me how determined she was to earn it."

"That explains a few things," Chad said softly. He winked at Andi to assure her that her disaster in the peach orchard would stay a secret, at least from their mother.

"Considering all you've been through these past few weeks," Justin said, "I think you paid an awfully high price for that gift."

"Oh, Andrea!" Mother exclaimed.

"But it was worth it," Andi hastened to assure her, "to see your face when you opened it. I'd do it again. I really would."

Andi's heart overflowed with gratitude to God for working "all things for good." The truth really had set her free. She'd earned her gift, Taffy was safe, she and Jack were friends again, and Johnny Wilson would soon be on his way back east—maybe not for good, but for a long time.

Could the day get any better than this?

Sure it could.

"Justin." Andi stood up and put her hands on her hips. "You're the oldest. Why don't you get busy and light the candles? I've been staring at that cake for nearly an hour, and I don't know how much longer I can wait to taste it."

"Spoken like a true Carter," Chad chimed in. "Let's eat!"

A literature unit study guide with enrichment activities is available for *Andrea Carter and the Price of Truth* as a free download at www.CircleCAdventures.com.

Contact Susan K. Marlow at susankmarlow@kregel.com.